Moral Compass

Coney Island, Brooklyn, New York

Rabbits once inhabited this island occupied by the original Lenape Native American Indians. They called the island Narnioch, meaning "The Land without Shadows", as the beaches facing South made an abundance of sunlight, hence the nickname "Narnioch" was given to it. With the Dutch settlers moving to this territory, the Lenape Native Americans sold the land to Dutch people, who renamed the area as "Konijen Island" meaning "Rabbit Island."

In those times, some parts of the island would reshape because of the tidal sand waves effect. Aquaculture and animal farming were considered to be a major source for surviving on this island. "Konijen Island" a name, once we all knew, reshaped to "Coney Island." This island, present-day Brooklyn did not stop evolving.

Coney Island became the place of origin of many great inventions. The creation of the initial amusement park in the 20th century attracted a lot of tourists. Inventors made their mark here too. With inventions like the Wooden Rollercoaster, Ferries Wheel the Carousel and, Nathen Hotdog, it was the Walt Disney of its time.

Chapter 1

———●(●)●———

Marc had the TV remote control in his palm. He was switching channels, one at a time. Overwhelmed, about the spaceship blueprints in his custody, he kept thinking, 'how in the world are we going to build an object that flies in the air? Which also possesses the qualities of a Dolphin.'

Sundara kept calling Marc's name in the background. His thoughts lingered on to the future. She looked at him while thinking of him. Marc shifted his head in her direction while gripping the remote control in his hand. Gazing at Sundara like a cave dweller. "Honey, are you Okay?" At first, she felt a little uneasy. She could see the remote control in his hands and heard the sounds of clicking while she was calling him, "Honey?"

He was looking at Sundara, lost. While she was talking to him, he was drifting in the realm of his own thoughts. What if her family didn't appreciate our daughter and me on Ooynt? While Laura was sleeping in the bedroom, Marc knew this was the proper moment to tell all that was going on. But little did he realize; her wife knew everything that he was about to reveal. She pretended like she didn't know to hone the new gifts that she had gained plus, she needed to discover the reaction of Marc.

"I have to explain something, Sundara," said Marc, and took out a marker and scribbled something on a sheet of paper. She thought to herself, here come the thoughts. He pulled out the blueprints, the ones he had shown her a long time ago; he wrote in bold letters. "We have to build a spaceship!"

1

She pretended to gasp, and wrote "What? Really?" he scribbled again, 'Yes, we have to build the spaceship from these blueprints." Sundara Hugged him tightly, and he hugged her back, like a little child who found comfort, after getting the big burden off his chest. She recognized all the details and thought about what was about to happen.

She glanced at his husband and wrote with a guilty look in her eyes, "Marc, I already know everything."

Astonished by the news, Marc was only able to utter, "honey?"

"Yes."

"What? How?"

"Reading thoughts of others is easy for me now. I don't know how long this will last, Honey. I couldn't tell you before because I didn't want to intrude. So, I waited for you to tell me yourself."

Marc nodded.

"Did Dr. Eugene tell you when he will call?" It startled Marc, "she knew!"

"We must wait for his message."

Two Months went by

Seabrook, New Hampshire It's January first, 2019.

The Brooks Family had bliss in their eyes. It's their first Christmas in their life where they had an unlimited amount of money to spend on each other during the Holidays... boy they did!

Brent and Margret Brooks wanted to make sure that their twin sons were not spoiled and that they learn about working as well. So, they bought this year two types of gifts for Christmas, working gifts and fun gifts. And they let them open the working presents first. They planned to capture these moments, so they made videos and photos while the twins were opening the gifts. The first one was two top of the line rakes both wrapped in same wrapping paper.

The Truper 26-inch leaf rake equipped with fiberglass handles which made it lighter. "Yes, my sons, you guys will still rake the leaves here," said Brent. Next, in the gifts, was a snow blower made with power smart 22-inch two-stage gas And John Deere D 105 with mulching capabilities riding lawn more.

Both Jared and Jarvis were surprised after opening the work gifts.

"Some gifts are from Lowes right here in town, and I could get a discount on a lot," said Brent. And for the fun gifts, he gave them each a gift card from Amazon for the highest limit of $5,000 on them a One-year gift for both...Two Monogram patterns skateboards.

A one-hour Helicopter ride over LA or Malibu with a photographer Both Margret and Brent accompanying them. "It was their first Christmas, and I wanted to go overboard on spending for my sons the first year." He explained to Margret. For his wife and himself, they both promised one gift each. She gave him a weekend on Yacht-the Dynamig, something which he absolutely appreciated.

And Brent surprised her with a planned trip to Hot Springs, Colorado. This place had mineral water pools which Margret had never experienced before, and this enthused him to arrange this exotic venture with his wife.

Walking back to the office, Brent opened the safe where he had two items, the relic handed down from the Indian Lenape Chief in New Jersey for the UFO trip. He opened the safe to look and shut the door of the safe securely. Even though, Nelson stayed near to watch over the family everywhere they went. He was a great bodyguard. The other item in the safe was "A Deed." His Uncle called him out of the blue and requested him to buy some specific land in Virginia of all places. He didn't tell his family about this secret Christmas present to himself. It's a Deed to an Island in Virginia.

This Island was on sale. "There will come a time where you will use this deed. Nephew, hang on to this, okay?", His Uncle instructed. He agreed. Sitting behind his desk, he delved into thoughts. I didn't question his judgment he knew the coordinates for the TV channel underwater. I trust my family. He is one of the few relatives who hasn't ask me for money. I wonder why?... Suddenly, there was a knock on the door, and it was Nelson making sure everything was going fine.

While sitting, Brent's phone rang, and he recognized the voice right away, "Marc? Marc Dazet? Is that you?"

Marc paused, and spoke, "Yes, it's me. Happy New Year to you and your family."

3

"Happy New Year to my reporter friend from Virginia... How it's going there?

"Well, Sundara and I were taking it easy here, each day at a time. How are the Twins there?

"I was wondering how excited they must be about this Christmas vacation, being your first Christmas together in a new sitting or, I should say nicer settings."

Brent smiled through the phone. "I promised myself to keep them grounded, its best to teach the teenagers their age about the work ethics, along with enjoying life."

Marc agreed. "Anything new on the relic, Brent?" This was the part of the conversation where both sides withheld information.

Brent said, "It is here in my safe? I look at it now and then, and put the mysterious item away.

"I would do the same.", Marc replied. There was another reason Marc called New Hampshire at the Brooks residence. It was a check in on his Uncle. Both parties were waiting on Dr. Eugene Brooks for answers.

"I haven't heard from him since 2018, before the new year" ... Sundara was watching TV while Marc was on the phone and she picked up vibes in their talks. She thought to herself. I can't make it out ... let's concentrate "Island" in Virginia what, why? Her senses told her. I'm not sure how true this is. I will store this small amount of information away.

Brent heard another call coming in, "One second let me see who this is on the other phone." He said to Marc. He clicked the office phone. It's the manager at Lowes thanking him for shopping there for Christmas season.,

"You can't take the Lowes out me. I spent too many hours there working" ...

"We know, Mr. Brooks.", said the voice on the phone.

"You can still call me Brent... There at Lowes. I put on my pants one at a time. Every day like you guys there."

"Okay, Brent," said the manager. Marc agreed with Brent. While listing in on the call.

"All I want to say is have a nice day from Lowes."

"You too."

He clicked back to Marc, "You still there?"

"I'm still here."

"Cool, look if I hear from my Uncle, I will have him call you back. Is there anything you want me to ask him?

Marc thought about it and said, "No I'm okay I'll just wait and see."

"Well, Marc we will talk again soon. Take care of your wife and daughter there."

"Sure, I will."

Brent thought to himself; I wonder what this year has in store for our family... I'm not sure if it can top the year 2017, as it was one of the most exceptional years of our lives... He stood up checked the safe a second time to make sure it was locked and walked out of the personal office space to look at his family.

Chapter 2

———————◆◇◆———————

Second Lieutenant Harold Johnson looked around his modern home for his family. And he couldn't believe they were assigning him on this secret disclosed Military base. He was sitting reminiscing about the time when he had the interest to be a fighter pilot. But eventually, things changed, and finally, the events changed as well. While they stationed his family to Germany, during the Eighties, he laughed to himself thinking of the individuals who supported him to where he is now. In all his ranks, his most prized one was the rank of being a family man. He was grateful for his family, his wife Hanna, and two children, Zelda and Nolan.

As his mind wandered in thoughts, something on TV caught his eyes. A woman was putting on a coat, and he stared at the stunning colors of the jacket. He could hear the TV in the background when she told everyone to buy the new YinMn reversible coat. What a tone, he thought to himself. It had the shade of purple and blue together. I never heard about this in Kansas where they actively assigned him, he thought. A visual wake up call. Hanna came into the room. "Hi Honey, are you Okay looks like you saw a ghost or something?"

"No, honey, I was watching this ad on TV about a coat, the color of the coat changes, and blends between the two colors.

"Honey," Hanna sat down next to him and spoke, "Honey there is a lot to discover here on the current base." Harold didn't speak he nodded back in agreement. He called the children in, to the same room to talk with them. "Okay, we are having our first family meeting." Zelda stared at her Dad and listened to every word he said, even at her young age. She knew their family

6

location differed from the past.

"It seems like we're about to start the springtime here," Harold told his family, although he wasn't certain what month it was. "It looks like the spring" Nolan spoke. "How can we miss Christmas here and the New Year? I don't remember celebrating Dad.". They all glanced at each other looking for answers.

Pacing to the room, Hanna did not like her family missing Christmas and the New Year; these dates were important for them. She walked in the dome home while she was talking, and noticed a scale button on the wall which looked like a sundial. Around the button were weather messages and Holiday phrases.

One label said Merry Christmas and another, Happy New Year. Then there were weather words associated with Holidays words. Something puzzled her about what she had learned. Words like cold, tropical desert, blizzard, mars and moon setting. There were two words that she could not recognize, one-word was Andromeda Galaxy and the other one, Triangulum Galaxy. She called Harold, "Honey, come here. I want to show you this object."

Walking over to his wife, he put his hand on her shoulder and said, "What's wrong honey?" "Look what I found over here. It seems like a Temperature gauge or some sort."

He looks at the device with some confusion. "We can't touch this until we talk with Colonel Mathews. He can tell us the function of this button." The children overhearing them, said something while secretly trying to look over their parents' shoulder to see. "We have to wait. Our moving truck should be here shortly to unpack. Let's Wait." Said, Harold.

Underwater, Yautja knew it was time to find the Relic Key. Now with clues, she had no time to wait. She thought to herself; I must go to New Hampshire and locate the key. She punched a switch, and a screen put the travel coordinates in as 32 Hudson Street, Seabrook, New Hampshire. It was a futuristic GPS for the Fiwusho people.

Moving fast to the entrance of the ship, she whispered, "I will be back." She advised the others who were in the space-time capsules, "I will unlock all doors." They couldn't hear what she said. She found the entrance, and thought could the same action happen for her while leaving?... then a loud noise as heard. The bottom twist opened, and there was a certain substance holding the water from entering, she jumped, and several lights beamed into the water. All the living water creatures disappeared when this happened. It seemed as if her thoughts dominated the ship movements.

Then the same force which carried her up carried her down. It was Yautja's mission to New Hampshire. While looking up from the bottom of the ship, she glimpsed as the platform closing and its lights going off. Then she went into a swim motion unrecognizable to the common eye. Swiftly, she descended in the water...

Robert has been working on the Atlantic Florida ocean for many years as a tugboat operator. Now, his job was to steer other boats out of crowded harbor's, towing them. These boats looked small but were mighty in engine strength. Their engines equal the railway trains of today. Robert worked for Towboats, US. In Fort Lauderdale, not too far from Pompano Beach, Florida.

He was travelling out to rescue a ship, and on his way, he noticed something in his binoculars. It looked like someone was drowning in the water. He looked again to make sure he didn't just see things. And yes, there actually was a lady necessitating help. He sped up his boat as fast as he could, and he yelled, "Hold on, hold on, I'm coming." As he got closer to her, she seemed lifeless, needing his help... he then cut off his engine and ran to the right-hand side of the boat, reached his hand down to grab her arm. And in this way, Robert pulled her into the boat.

She couldn't speak but just be thankful...Yautja didn't want to make a scene. All she wanted was to be near her car on Pompano Beach, Florida. She was now on Robert's Tugboat, getting closer to start her mission. In the meanwhile, Robert calls in the situation. The company was sending another boat for Robert's assignment. Yautja couldn't be happier for this help.

She noticed the speed of a ship; it was slower than most. She observed the tugboat keep moving closer to shore, but she added a slight twist by having the boat operator drive closer to her destination.

Robert stirred his boat toward the right side and headed towards the northwestern shore, waters away from Fort Lauderdale. He didn't know how this change of route took place. It took about 25 minutes to reach the right place for Yautja to jump off the tugboat, into the water closer to Pompano.

Robert went to check on her to see how she was feeling, but when he went to the front of the boat, he witnessed something unearthly. She released the blanket surrounding her and with a quick, lightening motion leapt off the boat into the water. Swimming at top speeds towards the shoreline …

Robert looked around in a daze. Getting back to the water location, Robert asked himself, "where am I?" He knew the coordinates very well, but he had never been here before.

Everything seemed mystifying in his Tugboat. He pulled his Global Ship Tracking Intelligence screen following the coastal traffic and noticed his boat was near to the Pompano Beach. "Why?", He said to himself. "And how? That's about 22.4 A mile away from the harbor water where I expected to be." He radioed in, to the main office. "Hello, this Robert calling," while calling in on his smartphone. The main person answered in Fort Lauderdale, "Robert where have you been, I've been calling you for a long time. But there was no answer."

Robert claimed he didn't hear the phone ring, "I know where I am, and you know Tugboat doesn't get lost in any waters." Puzzled, he said, "I don't know how I got here." The other person the phone told him, "Take your time coming back. Well, see you when you get back." Robert was still perplexed about what had just happened. He changed the boat south and went back to formula waters.

The shoreline looked right as Yautja was swimming near the ocean waters. She had noticed the area already, where her muscle car stayed parked. So that she could blend in more, she jumped out the water near the fences, not so far from her car. The gate was open as the passengers were coming on and off cruise ship liners. She noticed a lot of people wearing sunglasses that read 2019 on them, happy as they could be, for the New Year.

She saw her car parked, as before. And as soon as she saw the shape, she walked at a faster pace than most and hopped in the car. There was a GPS that she always used while she was on earth. She punched in 32 Hudson Street, Seabrook, New Hampshire. The GPS voice said, "The distance is 1506 miles, and it would take 23 hours and 11 minutes." She knew the meaning for miles and hours on earth.

It was a straight line up the eastern coastal waters. Her eyes gleamed; nothing could get in her way of finding the Relic Key at 32 Hudson Street…

Chapter 3

━━━━━━━━━━━ ✦ ✦ ━━━━━━━━━━━

The phone rang in Virginia Beach. It was Brent on the other end. "Marc, is that you?"

"Yes, it's me, Marc," he replied, *"You called back sooner than I thought."*

"Yes, actually, I received a call from my uncle." Marc perked up because he was waiting for some sort of sign for a long time. *"He told me to tell you he will call sometime next week; he gave a date. And he said to tell you the word Boomerang."*

Marc was startled to hear this word from Brent on the phone. Marc thought to himself, Boomerang, I wonder if he means I need to call him. He gave me a signal of calling him. Maybe that what that means!

"Okay Brent, Thank You for sending the information."

"My uncle is a mysterious person, isn't he?"

"Can you say that again? A mysterious person?" Marc agreed on both phrases.

The two parties held back information for the second time from each other like two lions who happened to be friends but can't speak. "Talk to you soon Marc," said Brent.

"Ok, Tell the Twins I said Hello and that bodyguard of yours too," the phone hung up, and Marc sat down with thoughts swirling in his mind Is it the right time to build this spaceship?

He opened the blueprints from the manila envelope and looked at them thinking they were purely fascinating, as what was drawn on the plastic slate could take them to other worlds.

As Marc was sitting, Sundara walked in to see how he was doing. "How is my Reporter doing today?" asked Sundara.

"I'm fine honey. How's our daughter?"

"She's fine. She will be home from school soon. It's their first day back to school from Christmas break."

"Honey, I have to go to the office to and see what's happening around the paper. Since we had a Christmas and New Year's, I'm sure a lot of the journalists are flowing in and out, working like Trojans," said Marc.

She left the room, and he was sitting thinking about how she became his wife and had their daughter Laura, his mind wandered. After college, in California their senior year they had their commencement speech, his mind flew into overdrive. I can't go to the east coast without marrying this young lady.

He had to think quick because in about two weeks before they would have to go their separate ways, and her separate way was another world. A long way from earth acting on his feet and making the right decision saved Marc. He thought of a plan. He asked her on a date to the ocean, and then, on the dune's hills of Pismo Beach.

He had planned well in advance. For two days straight, he wrote in the ocean sand with sticks. Each letter about 6 feet tall. He made sure it was far enough from the ocean water to not get washed away, what he had written. Then, the day finally came, when he dressed for the date and picked her up and went to the oceanfront to ask Sundara this life changing question.

She gave him a curious look, "Is everything okay?" He told her that everything was fine and that he wanted to have a date with her before they left the west coast. When they reached the ocean, she said that she loved the beach. They walked to the dune, the air was breezy, and the smell of the shells and the salty ocean water was more impacting today.

He told her to close her eyes before they went downhill off the sand dunes and she did. As they were walking, his heart was pounding in his chest, I said to myself, "Marc Dazet, this is going to be scary but also exciting, so you must do this. You have spent hours writing each letter in the sand." He thought to himself.

He then, told her to open her eyes, and she looked and stared for, what seemed to be a long time, absorbing the words, and he said to her out loud, "Will You Marry Me, Sundara?" When she heard this, her ears took another shape.

She was dumb folded. Marc ran down the hill and walked to each letter. And said out loud "Will" and then went to the next word "You" "Marry me Sundara?" He walked to each word to make sure she saw this important sentence. Sundara stood in a shock, and it took her a while to realize the whole situation. Because where she came from, this did not happen.

And then out of a sudden, she ran down the hill after him with joy and said gleefully, "Yes Marc! Yesses!!! I will Marry you." Both of them were so happy on the beach, with the words. "It was great... I did not know if this would work," Marc thought. She said out loud, "What do we do next?" He froze and did not want to think about what steps to take next. He was just so happy that she had said yes before she went back to her galaxy.

Snapping back to the present times in Virginia Beach, he had to get ready, to drive out to Norfolk, Virginia. Laura was back from school, she walked in and said hi and gave him a high five. "So how was the first day of school, was it okay?" His daughter Laura spoke with exactment, everyone seemed at ease today and kind of wanted to come back to a school, Dad.

"Yes, that's how it is when you're back to school after a break everyone wants to show their new Christmas clothes and gifts. Marc replied She smiled and understood. She too had new gifts that she wanted to show her friends, a new Apple watch and a cool outfit that her mom had bought. Marc was proud of his daughter adjustment to American schools in Virginia. He hugged Laura to say goodbye and grabbed his keys to leave the condo.

He walked towards his Jeep Cherokee and set out for Brambleton Ave in Norfolk. It was the end of winter in Virginia Beach, and it was less crowded with tourist. Having less traffic for a change was good. He arrived at the newspaper office in no time. He wandered by to Amelia office to say hi, she said, "Hey Marc, how were your holidays?" He told her they were fine as everyone needed the break.

After, catching up with his managing editor Amelia, Marc went over to his desk and sat there swiveling in his chair, thinking about new stories. His mind was stuck on a past story with Brent, and this seemed to consume his mind. But he still had to work here. Amelia called him on the phone, "Marc, look, I might have a story for you. You know, there are these bike trails, here in the Hampton's Roads area, for the whole state, could you find out more about what's happening and write a story about this?" Marc agreed.

"I am an outdoor person it would be neat to find out more about this case," he thought. Before he started his research, he wanted to call Dr. Brooks, who had told him that he could call him any time of a day or a month or year. He walked outside a little away from the newspaper building and took out his cell to call. He had to think and remember how he said to make a call, "I have put today's date, present day, month and year. So, I should dial 01 17 2019.

It rang for about two minutes. And the formula voice replied, "Hello Marc, is this you?" And again, with Time travel he didn't know Brent's uncle's present location and didn't recognize the noise in the background. Something felt new. He stood still gripping the phone. "Marc, I'm glad you called. My nephew said you wanted to talk me, and did you get my word Boomerang?" He thought to himself how did he know.

"Yes, I got it…"

"Marc, a lot is going on… I will explain to you what I can on the phone, and we must meet in Hampton, Virginia. I have given you a paper. There will be new people entering your life who are helpers for this mission of building the spaceship. Marc perked up. "I know them. They'll be getting to know you. I will tell you their names, one of them is Joe Lewis, not the famous boxer but a normal person and the other name is Tobias and the W.S. They're going to help with the project happen, and Brent is also going to be a big help and me too.

I wanted you to know their name beforehand. On the right time, these people will enter into your life so don't be alarmed when they do. Tobias is a time traveler like me, a gifted one. Joe Lewis and his partner bulldog will support you with transportation demands. Rest I will inform you later...I have to run now. Look, call me in a week and a half, I will be at the Langley Research Center, and then we talk more."

Marc stared at the phone and tuned in to the sounds of the environment he would probably never hear again in his life. "Okay Marc, see you in a week and a half," said Dr. Brooks.

"Okay Dr. Brooks," the call ended. Marc went back to his desk thinking who the new people in my life would be like. He was excited and cautious at the same time. Walking back to his desk his mind went into overdrive. He sat at his desk taking in the phone conversation from Dr. Brooks. Who's the W.S.? he thought. He picks up the phone, "Let me call Sundara and talk to her," the phone rang, and she picks up. "Marc, you're okay?"

"Yes dear." He answered.

"How are you doing?" She knew he had a lot on his mind. And she also knew, he wanted to tell her more about the new information that he had received. Moreover, she was aware of the details before he spoke. Marc spoke in code. He said there would be some new people entering their life. She went silent and wondered who these new people would be? Would they come to motive and help or hurt us?

"They're here to help us, Sundara. I will tell you more when I'm back home. I had to call to hear your voice and see how were you doing. Its Ok do not be nervous." He said in an affirming voice. "I should get back to work now, see you later honey, stay safe."

Both hung up from the phone. Marc sighed and typed in regional bike trails in Google, and there were the number and information of the director for Hampton Roads Planning. He called the number to find out more about the bike trails but received a voice mail. He spoke. "Hello, my name Marc Dazet, from the Virginia Pilot Newspaper, I wanted to speak to a representative about the regional bike trails in planning. Could you call me back 757-446-9001? Thank You." Then he hung up.

He went back to the website to get more information about the regional trails. It intrigued him, the planning. It took his mind off the major events in his life. The online story mentioned many regional trails, but his focus was on one called the Birthplace of America Trail. It seemed very catchy, but it was not built yet. The name and this trail, Marc wanted to know more about the project.

He wrote in his notepad, regional trail system, from Hampton Roads to Richmond. Great name, he thought to himself. Then he closed his notebook. On his first day back, he analyzed, "It was a short day with a lot going on." And now, it was time for him to head back to Virginia Beach...

Chapter 4

————————×( )×————————

Margret Brooks was still impressed from the UFO trip to Wanaque Reservoir in New Jersey. She was going through the pictures and gifts they had brought in from the Lenape Indian tribe. It seemed as if their lives had been changed after this trip even more. She wanted to talk with Rhonda, their tour guide, to see how things were going with her. She had her number, so she sent her a text, "How are you, Rhonda?" She replied right away, "I'm okay, it's nice to hear from you when you are you guys coming back?". Margret texted, "I wish to come right now."

She asked if she could call her, but Margret told she was much of a text person. Rhonda said, "I'm the same, but I'll call you." Margret agreed, she was excited, being a History teacher, she wanted to talk more about the history and trip. The phone rang right away. Brent and the twins were out riding around Seabrook, New Hampshire.

"Hey, how are you doing?" asked Margret.

"I'm doing okay. Miss you guys."

"Me too, Brent still has the Relic safe here."

"Good, I'm glad. We are a spiritual community. Our food, medicine, everything that we are doing here has a spiritual significance. Margret, our Chef, keeps many artifacts that even I have not seen, he is talking with the youth right now about the history of Wampum."

"What is Wampum? asked Margret."

"I will explain soon. I wanted the Chief to talk with the youth without me. The reason that I called was to know if you guys could come back here to New Jersey. I mean if you had the time again. I needed to show you something that I can only show you here. Anyways, how are the twins doing Jared and Jarvis."

"They're doing good, just finishing the holidays here. Yes, we came out of Pooxit and Winigischuch? The time for falling leaves and falling snow.

"Yes, we have Christmas here and the New Year as well."

"Happy New Year, Margret." Margret greeted her the same.

"Yes, I will tell Brent to come back there with the twins. It would be fun and informative."

"Okay Margret, I will call you back soon, deal," she agreed, and they both hung up.

Rhonda heard the Chief say to the youth. We are good hunters and fishermen. We make our own boats, and they're called Dugout Canoes. They are made from Muxulhemenshi trees (Tulip Trees). All of them shook their head knowing what the word meant. He went on and said that they burned the tree at the base until it fell. And repeated the process until a hollowed section would create the clearing. They made great boats for all types of waters, the Ocean, events, small boats, big boats all sizes.

North Atlantic channeled whelk shell and white and purple beads made from Quahog a hard clam made the base for Wampum beads. One of the boys asked, "What are the beads used for?"

"They were used to for trade for metals anything needed. They were so valuable that they developed into a currency and we made a trade like real money with these beads. We knew the waters well here on the eastern shore."

"Our Wampum beads are on strings like the ones I have around my wrists right now," said the Chief pointing to them. The youth saw many of the beads around their families, but they did not know the true meaning. "We use them for storytelling and treaties between us and the settlers. They took a long time to make the Wampum beads. The process is difficult. Only tribes on coastal waters had access to the shells you see today," he explained. They asked another question about the belts.

"Yes, this made to if a canoe had a Wampum belt draped over the canoe everyone knows there is a diplomat inside the boat and, not to mess with that particular canoe. This all for today; we'll talk more about it later, okay." They all stood up for the Chief as a gesture of respect. As the room emptied, the Chief walked over to Rhonda, and asked her, "Did you tell them? The Brooks family, for a re-invite? I must tell them something about the Relic." Rhonda replied, "I told them, Chief." With vexed expressions, he said, "Okay, good, it's important."

Jared and Jarvis, with their father and Nelson, were driving a Forrest Green Suzuki Jimny, speeding along the Seabrook roads. One may ask if there was a difference between the two twins. They were identical, yes there's the difference, one area that's unique. The difference is highlighted when one's spends time around them, Jared was louder and had more of a boisterous demeanor.

On the other hand, Jarvis was more reserved, quiet but not shy. If they were both in public, one could hear Jared's voice first, whether over some disagreement or in a normal conversation. Jarvis usually kept it to himself. If using a metaphor, Jared could be Rick Flare, and Jarvis could be Neo in the Matrix, always thinking and questioning. He didn't say much unless it counted. So, these were the twins, and one was an extrovert and the other introvert.

They were driving through town, and the first one who to speak was Jared. "It's the New Year 2019. It's the New Year! My Cowboys are playing as they are America's best football Team. Do you agree?" Jarvis sighs. Nelson was driving at the legal speed.

"You remember, you guys wanted to have an amusement park here, in Seabrook?" There was a glee in Jared's eyes, while he excitedly said, "Yes, I remember Dad." To which Brent said, "Well, I can't tell you all but, keep that idea in your mind." Jarvis, liking the idea, put his two thumbs in the air.

"Come on, Dad tell us, pleaseee?" Jared insisted. Nelson was looking around the rear-view mirror like he knew the plan, not from Mr. Brooks but from another source…

Jared said, "Dad you made sure where going to be working I notice with upgrading the tools... Yes, it will build character, Son. We do have money now but nothing replaces a good character."

He felt, working at Lowes for so many years had helped him out in getting along with other hard-working people in Seabrook, "My Lowes experiences will be the back-yard work and other adventures coming up kids." The twins looked out the window at the same time wondering about the other adventures.

Suddenly there was a sign and a parking lot. The sign read '99 Restaurant'. Jared said, "Yes! The 99!! They have great Burgers here." So, they decided to grab a bite there. While they were walking in, a member of the Free State Project was walking out. The man said to all of them, "It's the Brooks and Dun Band!" Brent said back, "Real funny, Harvey. How are you doing today?

"I am doing fine, make sure you try the Vermont Cheddar Burger," said Harvey howling like a wolf, "Woooo Weeee! it's good!"

Brooks and Nelson were hungry. Small talk seemed like a barrier to good food on Lafayette Road. It looked like they were running a football play for a touchdown. The 99 restaurant's door equaled the end zone. Harvey shouted back, "See ya at the next Free State Project meeting Brent."

"I will be there Harvey, take care and see you next week." while they put sevens point on the board walking. They found a table, and everyone ordered their food. Brent took Harvey's advice and ordered the Vermont Cheddar Burger and seemed thrilled. The bodyguard made sure they were not facing the window as a part of procedures in guarding the brook family when they're at restaurants.

Brent happened to look out the window and saw something strange by his car, and it seemed like a muscle car parked behind their car strangely. Brent tapped Nelson, he stood up and walked to the door making sure whoever was in that car saw him. Then suddenly the car backed out slowly and took off quickly. Jared looked up from eating and said, "Who was that who was that?" Jarvis was startled. He was looking at Nelson leaving their table in a hurry.

"They were quick," Brent said to Nelson, "Someone was stalking us." All of them went back to what they were doing, but an unsettling feeling hit the air. All of them were curious, thinking Who was that? The meal was served in no time. Even the employees at the 99 Restaurants were nervous as they knew Brent and his Lottery winnings, they also wanted the family safe. Brent asked for a to-go box, and he wanted his Burger, it was good. He then called Margret, "How you honey?" She told her that she was fine and that she got off the phone with Rhonda from the Wanaque Reservoir. Brent went on the say someone was following us here to the restaurant.

Maggie was worried, "What! Are you all okay, honey? Oh My God?!" She was panicking, but Brent calmed her down, "No, no honey, we're all Okay. Don't worry."

Jared, a bit disturbed, asked, "Dad, let's get out of here?"

Chapter 5

───────── ◄►─ ─────────

The Johnson's were waiting outside their new residence. The moving truck pulled right on time, at 1500 hours (3:00 pm) and the movers came out, Nascar pit style and unloaded the truck in their new dome home. There was less to unpack because of the no plastic item rule that they used to follow. Harold was amazed at the speed of the movers. Hanna was happy to see these things back as she missed chairs and tables, somethings never change. Zelda and Nolan would be starting their new school tomorrow. Here on the base

Colonel Mathews calls to make sure that all went well. Being a District Commander, this was his Job to make sure that his troops were settled in for their mission ahead. There was a neat sound that came from their Dome. It was a beeping sound, one of the movers knew what it was, he said, "You have a phone. Here, Click this button."

Harold did. He had a surprised look on his face. It was the first time that he took a phone with a device built inside his home. "Hello." The voice answered, "Hello, yes Second-Lieutenant Harold Johnson, it's me, Colonel Mathews. How are you doing so far here on Sahara command post."

"I'm doing fine. The kids start school on the base tomorrow." The commander stated the start of the schools here, differed from anything they have seen. *Anyways, let's talk tomorrow at the "Swarracks."*

"Does that mean Space Barrack?"

"Yes. How about early at 10:30 am, we can talk about the mission and start the training soon."

A noise came through, and it seemed like something got delivered. It was the mail, and it came in from a glass door as it opened. One could see it was the orientation from North Apex High School, both Zelda in the 9th and Noah 10th grade. The Crusaders and the colors were dark green and burgundy. The package landed in Hanna's hands through a system that they had never seen before.

It was a mailing system new to any Military base they ever saw. On the top papers, it said: "We Want to Welcome You to the North Apex High School." Zelda was listening in the background as the movers were unpacking, Nolan was looking at the new mailing system. Their father was on the phone with the commander, "Did you get the package yet.?"

"Yes, we got it," said Harold.

Hanna was reading, "There is a school bus that comes by until our son can drive on the base."

Harold was happy about it, while he was one phone and listening to his wife.

"See you tomorrow Sir."

"Okay, Col. Mathews." The packers completed their task. The whole family looked at their items with their new dome home in admiration and uncertainty. This base differed from all the stations that they had been through till now.

Harold told his wife that a lot had been going on there in a very little time as it seemed like they had been living there for five months. Hanna was reading the paper she received and explained to her children the bus would be in in the morning at 9. Okay, I will make sure you're ready to go... Both Zelda and Noah were excited and cautious about the first day of school in their new setting.

Their dad told them to go to bed early for tonight so that they wake up on time. He knew he would be up in the morning too. He looked at his uniform, "Space Marine Second Lieutenant Harold Johnson," and thought to himself when I put on this uniform tomorrow, and a new life begins for his family. Everyone sleeping when Harold woke up, he was always the first. He walked into what seemed to be the kitchen area of the dome and a voice greeted him, "Good Morning, Mr. Johnson."

He looked around to see who was in the same room with him. He could see no one, but then he looked in the corner a cool-looking coffee machine turned on. He couldn't believe, he poured the coffee in his metal cup and tasted a sip and thought how do they know how I like my coffee. Who told them? He kept sipping; this is the best tasting coffee that I have ever had. He ran with the cup to his wife, "Honey take a sip of this." Still half asleep she took the cup and sipped.

"Yeah, it is Good. How did they know about your coffee taste?" asked Hanna with surprise. Hers where two creams and two sugars. Harold's was different; he liked no cream and enough sugar where he could taste the coffee and sugar slightly. Looking Harold, Hanna said, "Let me give you cup back, you want it back." Harold held the cup back with childlike excitement, "Gimme that" and started drinking it.

He put on his new uniform with pride and heard the kids waking up for school. The living area was new for everyone. They knew this feeling, from moving to many Military bases in the past but this one was very different. After breakfast, he was ready to head out. He checked his uniform, the cress on pant even and in the right place, starched and clean and boots tooled. He kissed his wife Hanna and told the kids that it would be okay for your first day, "Just take in with stride, it will be my first day too. We will all experience the same moment. So, Hang in there, kids. Everything will be fine."

The door leading to the garage opened, and the light automatically came on. Harold walked over the Google/Ford electric car, unplugged the plug and touched his hand on the window and the car unlocked. He told himself I don't want to try all the technology with the car today, I want to make in to my first day of work okay.

He jumped in and the garage door opened to a separate garage area, and the car turned on, as soon his hand touched the glass window. He had the open choice to drive, or the car could drive him to work, but he decided to drive it himself. The car asked him his directions to which he said, "District Commander's office," and the car knew the address. While in the garage area, the second door opened, and he was out on the base. The car was moving along with the other vehicles.

It didn't take that long to arrive at the office there was a sign in front of the building that said,

"District Commander Colonel Mathews. Operation Space Sahara 20." He walked in, and a person saluted him while in the front entrances of the building. The soldier said, "The Colonel is waiting upstairs for you, Sir."

He knew what he had to do. In this building, to reach the floor for the meeting, he was to be scanned by an eye scanner and also for the handprints. Then he saw the glass doors where the Colonel was sitting, ready for the meeting, "Welcome, Second Lieutenant Harold Johnson."

"Hello, Sir." The lights went brighter on their own; he didn't know how.

"Have a seat. Have you guys got settled in your new home?

"Yes Sir, slowly but surely." I wanted to ask there is a button with different temperature and words on it, I noticed most of the words but what do the words Andromeda and Triangulum mean?"

The Colonel paused before he spoke, he used to choose his words wisely, "These are two distant planets away from the Earth. You will be trained in amongst many other procedures." Harold listed in and took mental notes. "Those buttons do not work currently, as your training advances the temperature on both planets will stimulate and conjure there at your Dome home when it the right time, it's all a part of training. I have said too much too soon. Later today there will be other army personnel from different branches of the military, meeting you for the first time. That is in an hour; everyone will be here so be prepared."

9 o'clock a bus pulled in front of their home, a modern school, but it was not a yellow school bus color Both Zelda and Nolan were surprised; it said "Go Crusaders!" it blanked the bus colors with dark green and burgundy. "Cool!" Nolan said out loud, and he wondered if there were other High schools around or were, they only one here on the Military base. The door slid open, and they walked in and found a seat. Everyone noticed that they were new in the school. The Bus took off, and they waved at their Mom slowly.

Chapter 6

D r. Eugene Brooks was back in the present time in Hampton, Virginia, busy talking to someone at a truck stop, someone named Joe Lewis, who happened to be a truck driver for the company called Rollins and Rollins. Dr. Brooks was speaking to him, "Look, I will need your help to transport the spaceship parts to a location in Virginia." Joe was a season owner-operator truck driver for many years. "Others will be helping you, but you will be the main person to bring this part. I have known you for many years. Rollins and Rollins helped with ordering wood for a certain base that we used for classified missions. So, you have to do the job."

Joe agreed, "I need to know the locations." He was a short man of 5'5 but smart and knew the truck driving business like it was the back of his hands. He was also aware of the roads and the interstates. Dr. Books gave him an advance payment, and it was more than enough for the trip. "Dr. Brooks, when will this start? Will I put the pieces of the puzzle together?" Joe had questions. "Not yet, the first part of this plan was to find if you would drive for us, Joe."

"Dr. Brooks, I have to tell you something. When I'm travelling there on the interstate, we have to stop at the weigh stations. At Radom times, in each state, there are weigh station, and they check the weight of the truck. The trailer has to weigh under 80 thousand pounds. Dr. Brooks, I wanted to make sure you knew this before we start this mission." Dr. Brook had his hands on his chain, and after thinking about this, he agreed to the weight size. "Dr.

Books everything under that weight is fine. when it goes over, we're in trouble," said Joe.

"Yes, I understand. This is a lot more than, you know, to drive an 18-wheeler what most people think. I will contact you again soon Joe," said Dr Brooks. Nodding head in agreement Joe went back into the Truckstop.

Yautja was in this town for about ten hours, taking the new surroundings of this North-Eastern shore town called Seabrook. She had never been here before. Although, being visited Boston, and Delaware previously, the weather and the accents were not alien to her. There was only one thing on her mind, getting the Relic to free her people on the Fiwusho spaceship which was stuck in the bottom of the ocean. Tapping the tablet in her hand, she studied maps and tracked information. The device tracked the Brooks at the 99 Restaurants; it worked quickly. In no time she was there, sitting in the car at a distance and watching as they walked towards the restaurant to go in and they talked to another man and kept walking, a bit faster.

They didn't know the Gentleman very well. Through their gestures and expressions, she could record faces and voices for her devices. This person stood talking with them for a bit, but it seemed as if they were in a hurry to eat. She needed a couple of minutes. There was a meeting that they "Supposed" to go, but the time and place were unknown. It was going to be a long process to retrieve the Relic, but the time was too short. It was her motivation. Questions started popping in her mind, how can someone have something that belongs to her people? Why would he have our Relic?"

She was staying at the Ashworth, by the Sea Hotel. It was nice to face the ocean here, in Seabrook, New Hampshire. The ocean kind of kept her more focused on her mission because it reminded her of the purpose of staying in the town. The front desk clerk looked at her for a moment thinking Is she from here? She looked different from most humans. Shaking off his thoughts, the clerk checked her in. Yautja knew this. It was like a routine here on earth.

Pulling out her device she looked through the gathered information. It listened intently to the voices and keenly observed the faces. "There are total four faces. Two older transcendentals and two younger transcendentals, which looked the same, people on Earth call them twins," the device informed her. "Hmmm," she thought "Twins." She began studying the information and thinking of her next move on getting closer without being seen. This was going to take a while.

She tapped the device to the spaceship, underwater, inside and out in the surroundings everything looked good, the fishes were swimming near the ship, curiously smelling the ship probably wondering about the big unknown object. It seemed like that in the device, by their movements swimming around the spaceship.

This intergalactic gadget was very advanced, with a single tap, it turned off. Then, she started thinking about her mission, like what could be her goal for today. Some of their warriors, the Wright Brothers in Kitty Hawk, North Carolina. The Brothers had to go to France for the approval for their invention. They have been there helping the brothers out behind the scene. France played a big part. She was thinking more on different angles to retrieve the Relic.

Margret anxiously welcomed them back in the house, asking, "Where were you guys?!" Jared said, "Mom, oh my gosh, someone was following us! And they want Dad's money!" Nelson thought I am going to keep a tight look on the family. Everything has been peaceful until today. I was wonder who was the one to follow them at the restaurant.

Brent quickly went to the safe in the office, opened it with the number combinations and saw the paperwork from the bank along with the Relic and his winnings. Staring at the Relic, he was thinking if they were in some danger. Also, the deed to the island was in the safe. The family didn't know about the Christmas present that he had bought himself. He did give some hints to his sons, but no one else.

Jarvis said to his brother, "Whoever it is, they are fast." Jared roared, "I don't care if they are fast or slow no one is going to touch our family! No One!" the whole house heard him yell. He was angry. Margret told him, "Calm down son, okay. We will figure this out. In the meantime, did you guys eat?"

"Not much," Jared said, "We were worried, so we brought it home in a takeout. Try Mom."

*"Well, let's all eat. You can't stress over an empty stomach, okay."
Jarvis went to wash his hands. He liked to stay clean. He was
hungry and wanted food to think about what's going on, quietly.
"Honey, is there anyone you talked to before today maybe you can
backtrack," asked Margret. Brent answered back from his office,
"No. I just talked to Marc in Virginia. We met Harvey at the
restaurant. All of us were so hungry we had to go in, we talked
about the Free state meeting, that was all. While we were sitting
there for about 20 minutes, waiting for our meal, we saw a muscle
car and someone was in the front, watching us. I couldn't make out
any faces or who it was."*

"How did you know they are following you guys?"

*"Because they parked right behind our car, honey. We waited there
for a long time. When we stood the person back, he pulled out and
drove off. Poof! Gone! in a flash. Why would they park behind our
car? The restaurants have two parking areas, one on the right and
one on the left nothing in the middle. We all stood up, the moment we
were walking out of the restaurant the car moved. The only person
to who we talked was Harvey, and we spoke for a moment, not long
enough, he was going out, and we were going into the restaurant."*

Nelson intervened and told the family, "You're in safe hands, okay? I will
let nothing happen to us...We need to be careful what and where we are
going." Brent made a firm statement, "I will not be a prisoner in our own
home and family."

Then suddenly, someone's phone rang, and they all froze. It was some new
ringtone. It had a cool beat. It was Nelson's phone, and the song was Panda
by Designer. Everyone was staring at him. Sheepishly, he told them, "Hey,
I like this song, Okay." He answered the phone and didn't move from that
room where everyone was standing.

*"Hello, Nelson. It is Dr. Brooks. How is my family doing? Just
pretend you are talking to a security supplier, so they don't know
it's me."*

They kept talking, and Nelson played along with the phone call, "Yes, I was
looking for modern security equipment. Then Dr. Brooks said, "Nelson,
be more careful around the family, guard them with your full devotion,

Okay? I will be travelling out of New Hampshire soon. I will tell you when you may hear from them about the location.

Nelson said, "Do you have a catalogue? You may send it. I'm looking for certain items." The family heard the one-sided conversation, and they were glad Nelson was more concerned about their security. In an effort to talk in code with Dr. Brooks, Nelson said, "I want to maintain an awareness of current trends and progress in your equipment." Dr. Brooks got it right away. He thought something happened or someone of the family was listening to him talk over the phone.

He told Nelson to answer in yes or no, "Did someone try to rob them?"

"No."

"So, did they hurt them?"

"No"

"Or follow them?

"Yes"

"Do you know who is it, Nelson?

"No."

"Okay, look if there is any progress. I will keep in touch more often." He thought, *more caution would be required regarding the plan,* *"Stay alert, Nelson."*

Nelson replied, "I will wait for your catalogue and watch for more updates on your website. Talk to you soon." The call ended.

Margret asked him, "Is everything okay?"

"Yes, I Just wanted to order more security equipment for the family." Jarvis said, "Yes, we are going to need it." Brent walked in the Kitchen to finish his food from the restaurant, and hugged Margret tightly and whispered, "I love You." She smiled and whispered back, "I love You too."

Chapter 7

—◆—

Marc was driving home in his Cherokee from Norfolk, Virginia. While driving, he was thinking about all that had happened, how dear his wife and daughter were to him and also about the new people he would meet. It was the month of January. The clouds were wavy, and the air seemed like it was in the 70s. He liked the weather of this time of the year, neither too hot nor too cold. And one could almost have the whole ocean to themselves. Tourists were scarce. One other reason the locals liked Virginia Beach was that it felt like a small town. It was a pacifying feeling when tourist season ended.

He arrived home at the Condo to his wife, Sundara. She looks lovingly at Marc and says, "Hi Honey Bunny." This expression came from a TV show as were most of her earthly words. At home, she made sure that she spoke American, most of the time, but she knew many other languages and customs.

"I'm doing fine, Sundara. It was great to be back at the office today. It wasn't much work to do, and a lot of people were coming in to the Pilot. Valley of Norfolk seemed busy, as more people were coming in. I'm not sure if more military families are being stationed here."

"I'm sure there is...," Sundara was interrupted with Laura's cheerful voice, she was back from school. She had come in the living room and said, "Hi dad. I missed you today," then she paused and said, "Mom... Dad, where do babies, come from? Today in class our teacher talked a little about the babies, and I was thinking did I come from?" "Reporters gene Marc momently thought.

Sundara said, "No honey, it is different for us, sit down and let me explain." Marc wanted to listen to her too because he knew a lot and Marc didn't know much himself if you know what I mean. Laura was not born in Virginia.

She was born in Ooynt, in the Andromeda Galaxy. "We couldn't have you born here on earth sweetie. Many people would have known who we are., "Laura, I had to go home for this to happen." Let me tell you how differently race grows on Ooynt in contrast to Earth. On Ooynt, we have four different life forms A, B, C, D. I'll explain to you here more simply," she said, writing on a paper.

"A" type are explorers, and they must be content with others who possess A-genes. I'm not sure if your Dad is A, B, C or D but, he fits another category, the one of the adventurers, just like me. Now Laura looked with close attention.

"B" type are the species who are gatherers, those who collect items, kind of like providers. These are like the farmers on earth.

"C" type are the warrior types, and they like to fight for a cause. They must marry another C, from Ooynt.

And lastly, there are the "D" types. They politically govern our planet. They are the diplomats or speakers form Ooynt.

Sundara then brought a holographic diagram. Marc went into shock, he knew about this before, but he was amazed at how it was explained. "Please go on," Laura asked.

"We can have three or many children at a time. Hybrid is the word for it. Or we can have one at a time. There are many from our kind who have Hybrid children living here on the earth and, many may not know this," Sundara laughed to herself while explaining.

"Another quality is that we can reproduce just like trees and plants." Everyone in the living room was giving Sundara full attention. Laura was absorbing in all the words and where she was born. Even Marc was learning as she explained how this was done.

"I had to go home instead of the Hospitals in the US. At home, they were more accepting than the Earth people. I went there by myself, without your dad. Then came back here with you, my precious angel. But it's better to tell your classmates that you were born in Virginia rather than Ooynt. You will have to answer a lot of if that happened Laura," she said cautiously.

"Your real name is Arual.

Sundara called her, "One day we all will go home to Ooynt, including your Dad too." All of them shook their heads in silence, imaging this intention to become read. One day.

With this, Sundara closed the hologram, and she hugged Arual and her husband, Marc. Then, there was a call on Marc's phone.

It was the mid-noon; a person had called. "Hello Marc, my name is Justin. I'm with the Hampton Roads Planning District Commission. I received a call about the new regional bike trails in Virginia."

This jarred Marc's memory, "Yes, Hello Justin, how are you doing? I'm the reporter who called about the project. I work with the Virginia Pilot Newspaper. Can I ask a few questions about the project?

"Sure, what do you want to know about the project?"

Marc and Sundara went to college in California, and they had seen some incredible bike trails before. He wanted to ask him about the style of the trails here for Virginia. Marc asked, "I saw one trail called, the Birthplace of America Trail."

"Yes, Justin said, "It is one of the many, but this trail was completed in 2015. A new one that we are currently working on is called the Virginia Capital Trail. There will be three types of environments that the trail will go through, the rural, urban and suburban."

Marc listened and wrote in his notepad for the story.

"And there will be several facilities to guide the travelers from one point to another."

Marc asked, "Would there be some pit-stops, I think they're called 'Parklets' or 'Mini Parks' along the trails?"

Justin paused, "That's a good idea. Yes, and it would give small business owners the chance to sponsor the mini-parks. It would be creative, and I will further Google this idea. In the meantime, the regional trails there many trails connecting each other, I will name a few of them. There's..." as soon as Justin said that, there was a call coming in from Brent.

He told Justin to hold, "Sorry, could you please hold for a second, I have to take this call." Justin agreed.

"Hello Brent, you're Ok over there?"

"Umm. Not exactly, I wanted to tell you that we had someone follow us to a restaurant here." Marc was surprised, "What?! Did you get a good look of his face? Did you try linking the car to Earth Surveillance Division?

"Nope, I couldn't; whoever it was, moved their face."

Weird, Marc took a mental note, "Look, Brent, you have won the Lottery there in New Hampshire, you have to be careful even more than before."

Brent then asked if he could fly there to Virginia, "I want to show you something."

Marc was surprised, but he did not disclose the information about building a spaceship.

He said, "Sure when do you want to come to Virginia? How about next week it will just be me then? And we can talk in person."

"Okay, next week sounds good. I have to go for a run. I will talk to you soon."

"Okay Brent, talk to you soon." Then Marc clicked the phone to Justin for the city. "Hey, can I call you back to get the rest of the story tomorrow?"

"Sure, after 2 pm will work for me," said Justin.

Marc took down his number, and the phone call ended. He walked out of the room with his notes for the story and went to his wife, "Honey, thank you for explaining this to Aural and me. I have heard and saw a lot of the events in person except for seeing Laura being born in Ooynt. While you were explaining in the living room, my hand was shaking after knowing about all that many people here on earth do not know.

"I love you, Marc. You are going to see this in person one day. Your nerves will be on high alert then," she laughed.

"Brent wants to come here next week to talk with me, Honey. I didn't tell him about the spaceship blueprints. But he mentioned that he had something that he wanted to show me. Plus, it's good he can have some free time, away from New Hampshire. It seems as if others know that he has won a lot of money. I worry that I will have to tell him one day about all that is happening and that he should be prepared for the others involved in the project."

Sundara hugged her, "Everything will work out, Honey."

Then, she asks about how the weather was outside. They both watched the weather on the news and had their personal weather report forecast from their condo. Since they knew more about what's happening than most.

Marc started the day off with good news for everyone in the Dazet house. While looking at temperatures, in the '60s with a dew point at a 38-degree, humidity at 42 percent, winds coming out of the Southeast at seven miles per hour. Sundara steps in and holding a device in her hand says, "Our regional temperatures in the area are about the same around the '60s and more and on Ooynt, the temperatures today are lower intra-cluster medium ICM's between the galaxies," Both smiles.

Laura went back to her room, thrilled and in disbelief of where she had come from. She would have to have a good way of explaining everything to her classmates or telling them that she was born in Virginia Beach. I will have to do with Virginia Beach as my birthplace for now. Arual put on her beat headphone and listened to earthly sounds from the device.

Chapter 8

―――――――◦( )◦―――――――

Hanna watched as her children Zelda and Nolan go on the bus toward school. She didn't know what to think, she had seen this common sight before on other bases, and she had had the same feeling that her children are safe, they are learning and not getting in any trouble. But there was an extra feeling this military base is unknown too many, there exploring the base. Just in case her children needed her on their first day of school.

An Hour went by, Second Lieutenant Harold Johnson was at the right meeting place. Everyone was in the same uniform. No one knew each other, and all had their military experiences from different branches. Then in the corner of his eye, Harold saw a tall person in uniform, he gets everyone's attention, "At Ease!" All of them stood fully attentive. With a loud voice, he continued, "Welcome to Operation 'Space Sahara 2.0', not 3.0 or 4.0 or 7.0. This is 2.0. I'm your new drill Sergeant my name is Backbone. Yes! That's right, Sergeant Backbone."

All of them held the words, and it descended on them that this person is going to be their new leader wheel there on the base. The Sergeant lowered his voice, "You have heard many ranks, backgrounds, and divisions in the Military but today you are all equal here, you understand!" All of them said back, "Yes Sir." Harold was through this drill many years ago before he was an officer in the Army. He was alarmed, but now he was on a different base, and the surrounding soldiers were all from different branches.

"I know you might be remembering the days when you had your first drill sergeant in your basic training. This is going to be your

second basic training," Sergeant said while walking through the line, facing each soldier, he said, "I think I smell something; I know what I smell the new positions! Everyone iron mike right now! That mean push-ups on the ground!" They all dropped to the ground and started the push-ups. The Sergeant roared the phrase, "Hurry Up !!!"

"On your feet!" Everyone stood on their feet, gasping for air including Harold. He kept thinking about what had he gotten himself into. He looked around him, all of his new comrades were looking at each other having the same thought. "Welcome to the Space Marine Infantry Unit!" he said in a loud voice, "We will study the future here... You will see things that you have never seen before, and your training will be the unique type of training."

"What you see here stays here and will be put to use when needed. There are three other people besides me who you need to know on name bases." All the three Commanders were there with the arms folded behind their backs, standing in a line of three each took their turn to step forward when their names were called out.

"Space bravo Backwards Commander Jorge Coleman... Space bravo Moon Division Commander Kristen Hernandez and Commander Jacob Scott from Space Bravo Water Spartans."

It was cool to see them in person instead of a video monitor all three commanders stepped forward and waved to everyone with sternness.

"Today in the building in front of you will be your barracks. I know each of you has your own homes. But while in this building, each of you will have an office and locked area to keep your written material away from home. This secret information and what you're learning here can't leave this building."

The building is called S.D Sahara Depot everyone.

"We will have Physical Training (PT) in the morning. Same place same time! OK? Everyone said, "Yes Sir."

"I can't hear You!" And all yelled, "Yes Sir!!!"

"See you morning soldiers." The sergeant stepped forward and walked away from the soldiers

about twenty steps and while leaving he said, "At ease Space Marines!"

Everyone went back to normal. After being a little relaxed, Harold looked around to see who was on his left and right. On the right, he saw the man with a name tag that said, Sub-Lieutenant Max Gonzalez and on had a patch said Navy. He thought, the same rank as 1st Lieutenant in the Army he is one position higher than me, nice. And to the left stood a female, her name tag said, Pilot Officer Bea Arthur and a patch of Air Force.

Her name sounded familiar to Harold, and her rank was the same as him in the Army at 2nd Lieutenant. He thought this is going to be interesting, stepping out of the line he introduced himself to both. They didn't say much but gave a vibe of agreeable people. Being army personnel, he didn't speak much either. Also, he thought, there would be plenty of time for them to get to know each other after all they were going to be there for a year. He didn't go into the S. D barrack yet, wanting to check up on his wife, he took a drive back home. So, he saluted both officers and walked toward his new Google/Ford electric car, jumped in and started toward home.

Zelda and Nolan enjoyed the bus as many other children looked at them as new. The school was not too far from their new dome home. Both of them were looking out the window. Their attention was on the ride to school seeing all the domes and new people around them. Absolutely loving the new environment and colors of the uniforms, they reached a massive dome building.

At its entrance was a sign that said, "Welcome to North Apex High School, Home of the Crusaders." It was great even the sign there was neat to them. Then came a big garage where the bus could drive in, the doors went up and closed once the bus was in. The garage doors led to another driveway. The older students on the bus knew what to do, they all stood up and stepped outside of the bus on the three moving walkways going into the dome, some moving slow, others fast, everyone jumped on to one sidewalk.

Both Zelda and Nolan had been to many airports, and it felt like they were at one again with their luggage, but this time, they were in their very own school, so they picked one of the walkways.

The flat escalators briefly shared school awards. The driveway walls were like a canvas of the school's achievement, it showed the won trophies and achieved milestones displayed electronically.

Other students stepped off the platform knowing where to go. Not sure about their stop, Zelda and Nolan stayed on until the orientation section came, and the walkways slowed down. They jumped off hearing the words "Orientation section Welcome Students."

There were students of all ages, from different backgrounds who had joined in on the orientation. They also walked to find each seat, they saw two in the middle, each folding down for them to sit. The room was resounding with chatter, till energetic music filled the place, and it was something like a fight song for the school. A female's voice was in the speakers, which seemed to be everywhere, on the walls, on the floor and even in our seats.

People of varying age groups were seated, and everything felt new. Apparently, many families were sent to this undisclosed base. Everyone was exploring the place, looking around astonishingly. Then the orientation ceremony began, and there was another voice introducing the ways of the school, "This school you're at today is more advanced but do not be surprised, take everything in.

When you are in your classes, you will meet new students. There are two types of schools. One type is called in-school and the other one, non-school, where you learn at home this would count towards your grades. The times of learning could happen at any time of the day.

The Orientation continued, and suddenly, students were showing up on the walls live, waving, speaking and welcoming newbies. There was a panorama view of students, from where no one knew. It was cool seeing them around the room. Nolan wanted to know if they were live, so he excitedly put his two thumbs up in the air at once, and the students actively returned the gesture. They saw each other and interacted real time. The kids kept thinking about how would their classes be at North Apex High School. After that, they sat down, and a speaker came, a middle-aged man wearing a jacket,

"Hi everyone, I want you to get ready to get a tour of your class area. Each year has its own section at school. We call the grades one at a time and your seat beeps when your respective grade comes up, so please leave the atrium and follow the moving platform to the right areas. Zelda and Nolan looked at each other surprised and a little sad for getting separated, "This is it?" to which Nolan said, "Look, we both have maps of the school in our papers so I will meet you at lunch and we will catch up there. Don't worry." She agreed, and her seat beeped at the announcement of grade nine, so she stood up and followed the paths.

Nolan waved at her. Then, the man announced, "Grade ten, please proceed to the sidewalk" with this he stood up and walked flat escalators and got off at platform number ten.

He kept moving to a section of the dome school. Everything was neat. Checking his map, he thought, yep there is the Tenth-grade section, and I can see the area for the lunchroom too. I am going to the right place. And Zelda also was getting accustomed to her new school.

Chapter 9

---◄ ►---

While the Brooks won a lottery, a lot had changed for better, but there also were some new threats in their life of others stalking them with intentions not known. He had to think more about himself and his family. Also, about every day, that what was in store for them. He was looking inside his safe where he kept the Relic, some official paperwork for the bank and most importantly, the deed. Yes, an agreement to a real estate area that he had bought and told no one about it.

Now his sons wanted an amusement park there. He thought it would be awesome to have it here, and I would be able to help the Free State Project and give my sons their dream park. He had the kind of money to accomplish all the tasks, after all, he had won 429.6 million dollars.

He took out a paper and checked the hallways to see if anyone was around his office in the home and carefully shut the door. Unfolding the deed, he read, "Starlings Island bought by Brent Brooks." Examining it word by word, he could not believe it was his. The location mentioned in the deed was the Pocomoke Sound, a part of the Chesapeake Bay. Brent read on the septic system was approved and installed. The island spread to 75 to 90 acres, which was a fairly big piece of land. The Twins would be happy for the size for the amusement park he thought and kept reading, and it stated that there was a village called Saxis not too far away from Starlings Island. He liked the name and decided to keep it as Starlings Island.

All sudden there was a knock on the door. Brent was startled. Not wanting to disclose this surprise yet, he said, "One Second."

It was Margret, "Are you okay in there?" she heard the rustling of papers from outside the door. Brent rushed to the safe to put the document back in and made it on time. The door opened, and he looks like a teenager hiding something yet not trying to get in any trouble, "H-h-hi Honey. How are you doing?" he said hesitantly.

"I heard a lot of noises. What was that all about?"

"I was just cleaning up some stuff."

She let go, "Okay Honey. I just came to ask, if you still wanted the boys to have trained with Mr. Atrushi for Mix Martial arts."

Brent blurted out, "Yes, I want them training with him for a long time. The more they can train, the better for their self-defense. He is a good instructor."

Nelson was in the background watching them both from the corner of his eyes to make sure they were okay. He had tightened his security with the family. It was not too tight, so they can't evolve but was steadier and more streamlined.

The twins were in the TV room. The room was equipped with surround sound and big screen, the brand Hisense 75-inch TV. It almost covered the wall. The NFL game was on, "Kansas City Chiefs versus Dallas Cowboys," Jared yelling at the TV for his team to have a better defense. The commentator stated, the Dallas defensive coordinator, Rodney Marinell, must play better to stop the Chiefs from running the ball.

Jarvis was in for the Chiefs. Both were so immersed in the game, and it seemed as if they were in the ground. Jared knew football like a coach on the field whether their defense was a 4-3 that's four down linemen and three linebackers. Jared told Jarvis, "The Dallas Cowboys are going nickel defense with extra defensive backs." Jarvis said nothing.

Assuming himself as one of the players of his favorite team, Jared went to explain, "We have always been good at the pass rush our front line. That's what makes us good to stop a run or the quarterback. Jarvis, it doesn't look like that happen on these set of down."

"Jared... I'm not worried."

Jared spoke back over the sound from the TV, "Did you know the Chiefs have two offensive conductors, two there splitting the duties of position Brad Childress and Matt Nagy. They are a tough team to hold down on offense."

Jarvis cheered for his team, "Go Chiefs!"

"This is America's team we are just watching the game, so sit back and relax...and remember this Jersey I'm wearing."

"Jarvis if your team were playing the New England Patriots or the San Diego Chargers then we would have been a game," commented Jared. Both brothers would do anything to protect one another and liked watching football but had two teams that were opposing each other. It was a Sunday afternoon. There was a commercial break, and Jared asked Jarvis, "You know, this Christmas was best one we ever had, in our whole life."

"Yes, we have an updated working tool. Just the trip by helicopter to the UFO sighting was near, in New Jersey."

Then Jared said in a whisper, "I overheard dad talking to a real estate agent in Virginia about something, not sure but it was something to do with some land."

Jarvis looked back, "Really?"

"Yep, he is planning something big. Do you think the amusement park idea is related to do this? Like in Virginia instead of New Hampshire?"

"There no way, Jared," scoffed Jarvis.

"I heard it! with my own ears, something big is going on.

"Okay, okay, easy bro. We must pretend like we do not know what's going on, when this happens or if it happens," said Jarvis and then they giggled.

While they were talking, Brent happened to come into the TV room, and they both straightened up, "Hi dad," Jared elbowed Jarvis. Brent asked them how was the game going.

"It's going well," they answered at the same time.

"Dallas is going to win," Jared said teasingly.

"Okay. We will see."

"Yes, we'll see!" exclaimed Jared.

Brent walked back to the kitchen area where Margret was cooking. She gave him a look of suspicion, didn't say anything but spoke with her eyes. He understood it was about the ruffling of papers and door shutting. "Honey, are you okay?" Brent asked.

She held up the okay sign in her right hand without speaking and smiled back. Brent opened the fridge, but paused to ask a question, "Honey I was going to an area of Virginia to speak to Marc, I thought we could all go there for a weekend trip just like we did in New Jersey. What do you think?" This question caught Margret off guard.

"I think it's a good time to step away from New Hampshire if someone is following us here. We can take a trip and come back on Sunday night. Oh, and I also have a surprise that I want to show you all there," he winked at her and got busy searching the fridge.

Margret said, "Sure let's go. I'll do the trip planning."

He went on and said, "I wanted to go to Virginia Beach and show you something, near that area where Marc lives."

Smiling she said, "Okay." She knew this had something to do with the noise in the office. Margret had always known her husband well, with a lot of money or without it.

"Good, then its plan. I'll tell Nelson about it and the helicopter pilot we used for our previous trip."

Margret couldn't keep the news to herself. She had to tell her sons.

"Jarvis, Jared, come here to the kitchen."

Both didn't want to leave the football game they both snored at their Mom for calling them. And they walked to the kitchen. "Yes, Mom."

"Well, we are going for a trip next weekend to Virginia. What do you think? Are you guys excited?"

43

Both looked at each other with wide eyes and in almost hysterically hand and arm movements. But corrected themselves quickly, they didn't want to show that they kind of knew what was going on.

"Virginia? We've never been to this state before. Although we have heard, it's the 'Home for Lovers'." Twins broke into laughter.

She laughed and said, "We're not going there to find your girlfriends. Your father has a surprise for us there."

Jared knew right away what he overheard in the office a few weeks back, "This must be it!"

"Sure, we would like to go."

"Please pack on Tuesday then, okay?" their mother asked. Both agreed.

"Okay, you may go back to your game now."

Both walked slowly back into the TV room. It seemed as if the news of the surprise was more important than 'Dallas Vs. Kansas City Chiefs' football game. Jarvis said to Jared, "You were right about the land idea."

"Yes, I know. I told ya!" Then they did their signature handshake which was only theirs.

Brent opened his safe again to check on important items. He happily told his wife and sons about the possibility of a new horizon.

Chapter 10

—⚬—

Dr. Eugene Brooks was sitting at his office in Virginia. Looking over his to-do list, he crossed-off the next line on the list. The upcoming task was, talking to Tobias in 2048. He stood with some paperwork, a watch, and a device and walked out of his office at the Langley Research Center in Hampton, Virginia. Grabbing a brown paper bag from his car, he set the gadget for the year 2048. After stepping out of his car with the device in his hand, all of a sudden, his whole body dissolved, with everything in his hand, an Indiana Jones satchel wrapped about his side.

His goal for visiting in this year was to find someone named Tobias. The advancement and technology indicated that he was in the year 2048, as in front of him was the garage-looking thing which moved sideways and up and down. There was a digital sign reading, 'Langley Research Center,' he walked in the garage and saw a person there, with red Einstein hair who was talking fast about numbers, figures, and formulas. Dr. Brooks called out to him, "Tobias, It's me Dr. Brooks from 2018. I need your help with a project."

Tobias was so into the work that he didn't hear a thing that Dr. Brooks said until he saw his shoes and stared at them thinking I know these shoes are not modern and he looked up surprised and said, "O Hello, Eugene! What are you doing here? How long have you been here in the Laboratory?"

Dr. Brooks was a bit tense about the mistiness. Tobias said, "I think when you traveled you weren't in full form so I couldn't hear you."

Both of them talked over the desk. Dr. Books continued speaking, "Tobias, I need you to help me build a spaceship in the year 2018. I want you to locate the parts that are needed for building it. You're the only one I know who can do this. You know how to read blueprints and also what can work in varying atmospheres and time zones."

Tobias paced the laboratory thinking while Dr. Brooks kept talking. There are others who are involved in this plan, from Virginia and New Hampshire. They don't know it yet, but they will help you build this."

"Dr. Books, I can't stay that long in the past, I have a time limit to follow. If I stay long, then it can alter the future and things might go wrong. I would have to think about it and get back to you on this. It's very important that I make the right decision on this Eugene."

Sometimes out of nowhere, Tobias would talk to himself in his mind, gone so deep in thoughts that he couldn't stop talking about numbers, words, and dimensions. "Time is not something to mess with, Eugene, others moved time forward and backward in 2018, but here as you know, we move time many hours ahead and back."

"I need an answer from you soon, Tobias. It is very important. I have a truck driver who will move the parts to a location where the manufacturing of spaceship would take place for testing for this assignment. We can't do this without you. I must go now." Dr. Brooks wanted to leave as soon as possible before Tobias would change his mind and said no. So, he walked out of the garage area. Setting the device for 2018 again it didn't take him long before dissolving back to 2018. He was back in Virginia, near the research center. He looked around to see if anyone saw him and he was stood clear this time from being noticed. And so, he crossed another task from his to-do list.

Yautja in New Hampshire was driving around Seabrook thinking about her next move on how she could find the Relic. The weather reminded her of Folusho. The weather there used to change regularly, more rapidly than on earth. She was in the hotel, facing the ocean, thinking more of the spaceship in the water and what would it be like to have her ancestors free once again, enjoying their normal lives, petting their pets, how would they react to see her again? But who knows how many centuries would the whole process take?

She pulled the map on the wall, and it showed a diagram of the city. The areas were marked of her position and the Brooks at the 99 Restaurants on Lafayette market. The Free State Project was a potential area where the man might be. She went through the recordings and observed all the faces. Her species could read minds and explore thoughts. She pointed to Mr. Brooks, and his ideas were like an open book to her.

Something came up that caught her attention. It was the word, Virginia. She was wondering what was going on in Virginia. He must plan to go there for something. She stored the thought. Okay, I know what I do. I need to find out when they're going and who's going. Is the whole family going or some of them?

She decided to make her next move after they come back from this trip. In the meantime, she devoted her time to studying them more, their ways and thoughts. She pulled up the Twins from the recording. They amazed her how do they have twins here like my planet? Some of them could have many at the same time. She looked at more thoughts from that day in the restaurant; most of them were of no use.

She pulled up a map to Virginia to know how far it is from New Hampshire, and a screen came out showing 678.8 miles indicating ten hours' drive in a car, the flight time of 1 hour and 33 minutes if the plane goes at 500 nautical miles per hour. She looked at the numbers, takeoff, and landing would take about 30 minutes depending on time. The research was all in an account of her plan. Yautja wasn't sure if they're going to Virginia, she has a good idea they are soon.

Then she clicked on the underwater view at the ship, to check if there was any trouble in the water or on top, but all seemed safe with fishes swimming around. She looked in the ship and different areas of the map room, being new it took her a little time with the directions of this mass spaceship from the Fiwusho planet. Everything folded away and stored. Everything was based on her making sure this relic was back in her hands period.

47

The blueprints were on his desk at home. Sundara and Marc were staring at them trying to see if it makes sense. She thought Whoa! This is going to be a nice size spaceship. I wonder how it will travel in the water and the air. She knew it is possible. The words on the blueprint were 'first stage cross-section,' on the top right-hand corner and at the bottom, the words were, 'Galaxy Trinity First stage,' "What's that Marc?"

"I don't know. I have googled these words online, but not a single word of that phrase came up. This is not from our planet, honey."

"It's not from my planet either," Sundara added, "I know it is important and this fell in our hands for a reason."

Marc kept thinking, "We need a large area of land to build this and water too. I'm not sure how we're going to do this." Both knew the impossible could be possible.

Honey, I forgot to tell you, Brent wanted to come down here next weekend to show me something. Sundara became concerned, "Really? Honey, isn't that kind of risky? Him coming down here to meet our family in person? Don't you think?"

"Well, I thought I would go alone to make sure everything is safe. He wanted to show me something. I'm not sure what. He is coming here all the way from New Hampshire. He is a good friend. I trust him a lot. Also, I will be able to share more explicitly here. We will be fine, don't worry. We've done this many times before too while meeting others." They both laughed and were serious at the same time.

"Remember that dinner function we had to an attendant for the newspaper? I thought for sure some people knew. I was offered a drink, and it didn't settle with my stomach, at that party Marc. Some others who saw me knew I wasn't from here by the way I was acting at the dinner function." She said.

Marc goes to say something, "Sundara we will stay close so no one can feel that you're not from here. Sundara I was drunk for a week from two drinks at that party." Then a text came from Brent Brook, "It's me, Brent." The Beep came in Marc looked at his smartphone and replied, "How are you doing and when you are you coming down to Virginia?"

"I thought next Saturday we were going to bring the whole family by helicopter, so we reach there easy and quick."

"Great." Marc texted back.

"You will meet the whole family and the twins too."

"I wanted to ask would it be okay if you give me a hint about the surprise."

"I can't," the reply came back fast, "Not until we get there. It wouldn't be a surprise if I told you   my reporter friend."

"Okay, then see you next Saturday, Mr. Brooks."

"Nope, It's Brent. We're friends now."

"Okay, Brent see you next Saturday."

Chapter 11

———◄ ►———

Hanna was at home, waiting for everyone to come back. She was patient but at the same time worried for everyone. The kids had their first day at school and her husband had his first day on an undisclosed military base. She had done this many times previously but this had a different feeling each time.

First one of the crew to come home was Harold, who came through the entrance door and hugged Hanna and said, "What have I got us into honey." She said

"It's going to be okay."

"I met our drill sergeant today; his name is Sargent Backbone. He reminded me of my first boot camp when I got enlisted in the Army. It was a real flash back."

Hanna looked surprised, "Really? But you're an officer."

"Not here, honey. There are many officers of different ranks from various branches. I made friends with a Navy officer, Max Gonzalez, and a female air force officer, Bea Arthur."

"Bea… I feel like I have heard of that name before somewhere not sure yet."

"We met after doing push-ups on Backbone's command, he doesn't play honey. I have PT in the morning at 9am. As I was telling you about the camp, officers from all ranks were doing push-ups."

All of a sudden, there was a beep. It seemed like Zelda and Nolan were confused on how to get into the home. It was their first time coming back to a home like this. Both were outside, waving their hands on the digital monitor systems. Hanna could see them from inside looking out one of their windows. Harold went outside to show them how to get in. It surprised them to see their dad home so early, "Hi dad, how did you get in? We have been out here for ten minutes."

Harold told them to put their thumb on the scanner and hold it there, so it can read the input or align their eyes with the monitor and hold it there, so it can read it.

"Okay Dad. both understood."

"Now, try it out to see if it works for you." Zelda did the process and the door opened. Then it was Nolan's turn.

"Let's try again so you get it, I will walk in from outside." He wanted to make sure that they knew how to get inside if Hanna or he are not home.

Finally, coming in both were excited about telling their Mom and Dad about their first day of school. "Just Wow!" Nolan said, "There were movable platforms thought the whole school to get in to go to classes, you had the option to walk but you could walk on the platform too. It was great!"

They told they had non-school classes and in-school classes together. It was different here. "Where are we Dad? Everything here is so advanced and modern. Will we stay here only for a year?" asked Nolan. "I wish we can stay longer than a year. I wonder where going to send us next? Would that place be more advanced than this?" asked Zelda excitedly.

Hanna and Harold were thrilled to see the children excited about school for the first time in their life. Most of the time they receive feedback as "Okay, it's time to go to the boring school again." But this time, it seemed as an adventure for the kids.

Everyone was talking at the same time because they were excited about their first day. Hanna took notes about what was everyone saying, she stored all data as if being a mom made her brain work just as she possessed the processing speed of ten computers.

"Honey, I can't believe we do not have plastic here at the base but only wood and mental," Harold noticed this on the base.

"Okay, now it's time for making dinner." So, they strolled to the kitchen area. "Cooking without our plastic," she looked at her modern kitchen, trying to figure out the new items that surround her. There was a bamboo table, it was equipped with advanced elements. When Hanna took out celery from the refrigerator and put it on the table, an amazing digital circle popped up and said Corral and listed recipes that could be made using celery. She was astonished.

Next, she placed some tomatoes on the bamboo table and the same thing happened with the digital circle with suggestions on what to make with the ingredient. She called the whole family in the kitchen to see this. They all were amazed too. She went back to the table strolling in awe. There was a button for video recipes of the celery. The video used to come up on how to cook a certain dish when needed.

They were all used to watching Go Flavor Go and other channels for cooking shows on the TV but here, all the help was available in the unique table. The Johnson family tried each new item. Harold was a good cook and he was thrilled even more for cooking in this modern kitchen. He told his children to put their school bags in their rooms saying, "Go on kids, put away your bags, there is going to be plenty of time to test out other features of the kitchen." As soon as the children left, both Hanna and Harold excitedly started exploring new features of the kitchen like children.

Max Gonzalez was stationed to the space marine infantry but this had quite a story behind it. He belonged to Sacramento, the capital of California, where a lot of laws are complimented for the whole state. This was where Max grew up. The reason why he was the right pick for the space marines' infantry was that he was brave. When he first joined the Navy, he was stationed for IT computer classes in Pensacola, Florida. At the time many who saw him had the impression that he was really into his studies and book reading.

One day, a peer of his said, "You never go out, you're such a nerd." But they didn't know which city he was brought up in. He said, "No I'm not. I can party really hard." So, his peers bet him on a drinking contest that he would go out with them and get drunk, any day of the week so Max accepted the challenge.

It happened on the weekend. They went to the beach, drank many pitchers of beer and then went to the other place and drank more. Also, he won the bet but there was more to the story on why he was selected.

They took the taxi back to the Naval base. And when they got to the gate him and his Navy friends were coming back and as he entered the gates, he saw senior Navy soldiers in the towards him. When they stepped out of the taxi, he was called by the soldiers. Max was partially drunk and in Navy if one gets caught in such state on the Military base, they can be kicked out of the Navy at once. At that moment he had to choose to turn around to see what they want and get kicked out of Navy or to run away and hide till he gets sober.

He chose the latter and reached out for his wallet including his ID and handed over to his friend in the taxi. He decided to jumped out of the taxi and told his friend, "A man's got to do what a man's got to do", and he jumped out of the taxi at top speeds running. On the base, not too far behind him, the group of senior Navy soldiers ran after him too. It was five soldiers of them running after Max. Five soldiers later added five more soldiers chasing him throughout the Naval base. Max sprinted so fast that he lost one of his shoes.

He ran to the wooded area of the base to take shelter from the soldiers. While in the woods, he received a phone call from his roommate, "Oh My God! Oh My God! they are chasing someone on the base about twenty people running after someone you should see it."

The roommate asked on the phone, "Why are you breathing so hard, Gonzalez?"

"They are chasing me that's why I can't catch my breath. Can you come to the base to get me out of this mess.?"

"What's that? You are the one they are chasing?!"

"Yes, it's me," he answered back panting. Then the roommate thought about a plan for getting him out of this situation. "Look

you're going to have run over the side of the roads, then I can pick you."

So, wearing just one shoe, he started running out again to reach to a car, with about twenty to thirty soldiers looking for him on the base. He found Max, and he jumped into the car. But all sudden, there was a motorcycle behind the car. Both noticed that it was one of the friends on the beach. The motorcycle honked for them to pull over and told Max that he had his ID and wallet, and that he was safe. Now, years later, the person he made that bet with remembered his bravery and he picked him for the Space marine infantry.

Chapter 12

—◀ ◆ ▶—

Everyone was packing for another helicopter trip, this being their second one since the last one was a year ago. The family, including Brent, were thinking, we're going to Virginia, a state we have never gone before.

Jared asked, "You mean they are on the Atlantic Ocean, like us?"

"Yes, they are. We are going to a bigger ocean with area eight times larger than Seabrook." The twins were taken aback by this information. They had done a little travelling to another ocean town. "Yes," Brent said, "The area of the ocean there is called Hampton Roads. My reporter friend, Marc and his family live in Virginia Beach, which alone is home to approximately a half million people. We are a tiny community of around 8 thousand in comparison to Virginia.

"Yes, we are going to a bigger ocean city... It's not that cold as here in New Hampshire. There is an ocean like here, the Atlantic Ocean same coast as ours."

"How long are we going to stay there?" Jared asked.

"Just for two days, but we could stay longer. It's not final yet."

Margret was checking around for the rates and where they wanted to stay, she liked planning the road trips. Brent asked her to choose an area called Yorktown, which was about 1 hour away from his surprise, only at 41 mile's distance. It was close to Virginia Beach and the area where the Island was located. Not too far where Marc and his family could travel, and visit them.

Margret googled Yorktown and saw that this area helped with the American Revolutionary War and other historical facts about the town. She liked more history and the fact that they will get to see all that in person excited her. She chose a bed-and-breakfast located there, called Marl Inn Bed and Breakfast. This stay at an inn was going to be a new experience for them. She called to make reservations for two days on church street in Yorktown, "Is that fine honey the distance and all?"

"Yes," answered Brent, "I'm glad about the arrangements you make, you put together great travel itinerary." Brent had a plan to pick up Marc and his family in the helicopter and bring them to the island, once they reached Virginia Beach

Jared and Jarvis were excited about the trip since they kind of knew what was it going to be. Also, they wanted to get away from New Hampshire, as they were being followed by someone. They knew that their Dad had won the lottery, but they didn't know how it can be a possible threat to their family.

"It's not a UFO trip, Jarvis," Jared told his brother, "but it is something new, something that we have never seen before and I like the feeling. Is there an NFL team in Virginia?"

"No, they have the Washington Redskins there, I noticed they have a native American Indian on their helmet. I wonder why?"

"I heard they were previously Boston Braves, then changed to Boston Redskins and now they are Washington Redskins," said Brent after overhearing them.

A skill he learned at Lowes was to overhear people's conversation and pretend like he wasn't listening to them... "Yes, not too far from here in Massachusetts. Just like the Atlanta Braves were from Boston Braves, first go came from Go "Tomahawk Chop."

"Great sports insight Dad," remarked the twins.

"Yes, working at Lowes, you learn a lot from customers in town."

Jared and Jarvis excitedly continued packing their items for their two-day trip. Brent made the call to the Charter Helicopters and spoke with Mike on the phone. He agreed for their second travel adventure and decided to keep all the information he sees, confidential. Just like Wanaque Reservoir trip what he saw there, remained unsaid, "Yes, I will Go, Mr. Brooks, how long are we staying for?"

"Two days, just the weekend there and back and we will be picking up a family from Virginia Beach. I think we're going to need a bigger helicopter if you could arrange it."

"Yes sir, we do we have bigger ones for all needs, but this will cost you a bit more. Like you don't have it," Mike said back to him smiling. He wanted Brent to know about the cost.

"Okay, we'll go see it on Friday morning." Everything was ready, but there was one more call that he had to make. This call was to the groundskeeper of his island, he called and told that he was coming down there with others for the first time, the conversation was short and to the point. Brent didn't want his family to know about what was going on.

Outside of the security gates a figured roamed the area of the Brooks estate. Yautja was trying to find more information about the family. She had traced their address from doing a lot of research on pictures and voices that she could not get much information previously. From observing them, she learned that the family was about to go somewhere, she told herself I would watch the plan go into action and I'll when they return from their trip. I'm not sure when they're going. I wish I had this information.

She saw an intercom system on their home. She thought this must be a way for others to enter their home. She was there to gather information. She noticed a car pulling up with an Asian man speaking into the intercom... "Hello, this is Mr. Atushi (Correct Spelling) he was the Martial Arts Instructor. "His voice is different," said Yautja overhearing him, "He is from someone where different."

"Come on in Sir," they made sure he was who he was, and the gate opened he parked his Toyota Camry and walked to the two doors of the three home. Mr. Brooks was waiting for him at the door he seemed to bow at him when he greeted him at the door, "Hello Mr. Atushi."

Mr. Atushi bowed back, "How are you, sir? I wouldn't be alarmed but there was something in the woods, looking at your home, I noticed while talking on the intercom system." He was fantastic at sensing others. "Mr. Brooks it wasn't an animal. It was something else."

Brent was a bit concerned, he jogged his memory to the incident that happened at the 99 restaurants, where there was a car parked behind their car. He stopped Mr. Atushi in his tracks while talking.

And called Nelson through the walkie talkie, it took him two minutes to search, he was patrolling the entrance gates of their house. After a while, he reported back to Mr. Brooks, "Everything seems clear here, Sir." He walked with Brent and briefed him about the updates around the security around their house.

Mr. Atushi waited to talk with Brent. He helped by describing what had he seen in the bushes. "It was really settled in the bushes, what I saw a normal person would have easily overlooked... I saw something blended in the trees."

He rushed Mr. Atushi in the door, as soon as he heard that, "Come to my office, let's talk about I in there." Both of them waved at everyone. The Twins were happy that he was there and stood to bow at him first. He paid his respect by bowing back and said, "I will be back. I have to talk to your Dad."

The door opened, Brent sat down with Mr. Atushi, "I wanted to tell you something... I'm about to start working on a project in Virginia, and I wanted to know if we build a training hall."

"Yes, a Dojo in Virginia would like to train the twins," said Mr. Atushi, "If they're here in New Hampshire, I can train them, and if they happened to be in Virginia, you could get them trained in a Dojo. I could help with the design of the Dojo, Mr. Brooks. I would like that a lot."

"Yes, you could design it from the ground up, if you would like, sure. We are going out-of-town, and we'll return in the next week. I will contact you Mr. Atushi when we get back. I just wanted to ask you in person, before going with the idea. That was smart to ask me face to face. It is the right way to do certain things in life."

"They will need all the protection in life, Mr. Brooks. Japanese martial art is not about defeat or victory. It's about shaping your 'Tai Sabaki' and

'Kiotsuke', or you do not learn to use the body movements and stay alert and attentive. It will be an honor for me to be their Sensei," he said with a heavy Japanese accent.

Then, Mr. Brook stood up first and Mr. Atushi too, and they bowed before each other which seemed like the end of the conversation. Both walked towards the door, and Mr. Atushi stopped to say hello to his future Yudansha. "I never explain to anyone what that word meant," he said, and the kids agreed. Jared said, "I couldn't wait to be in your class learning from you."

"It will happen soon, I hope," he said, "Okay, I must go now," and he walked out of the French doors heading towards his car. He drove out of the gated driveway. He could still feel the same presence in woods near the home, but he kept driving.

Yautja was still there to see if she could have any clue, but everything seemed airtight tonight. She added a new person to her investigation, man of Asian descent. She got back in her Muscle car that was parked away from the Brooks home out of human sight, of course. On returning to the hotel with her notes, she had only one thing on her mind "The Relic."

Chapter 13

———————×( )×———————

He had been driving for Rollins and Rollins as a truck driver for thirteen lengthy years. He accomplished some special, conventional assignments and some rather anonymous and unconventional ones too. He successfully executed all of them.

Joe recalled the time he used to study in a truck driving school to get his Commercial driver's license in America. It took him 30 days 160 hours in total, he had to clear a verbal test and a skill test before he received his license. Joe passed all the tests.

He preferred to be an owner operator of his own truck so he could have more freedom on the road and more money for himself. Normally, being an owner operator, one had to pay for the fuel out of their own pocket which was reimbursed by the payment from the taken job. This was why he chose Rollins and Rollins, he did his homework on the company and knew they would pay him for gas and fuel, before the trip started.

When he drove, he followed strict timelines and made sure that everything was on time. Rollins and Rollins provided their services on the eastern coast, which was a highly paid route. It was a perfect fit for Joe. With the experience of 13 years, he knew the terms and the circumstances of the interstate very well.

A truck driver delivers many items on an 18-wheeler, traveling from state to state, from country to country delivering goods and services for the same, many long hours daily. These delivery services are the backbone of any livable place today. Think the big screen TV, laptops, electronic gadgets, drinking milk, all are delivered by a truck driver. Joe felt that despite working for many years, people never stop to think about all the effort that is put to deliver these services that they buy in malls and marts.

Joe liked driving, he knew that his job legitimately supported others like a firefighter, nurse or teacher but his job lacked appreciation in comparison to other jobs. People hardly stop and think where their daily use items like pen or paper come from? But this never kept him from serving people. The company he worked for and Dr. Brooks needed his skills and they would pay him in whatever amount he decided.

Truck drivers have rules to follow on a daily basis, firstly, by law they are obliged to drive 11 hours a day with, small breaks for rest, fuel breaks and eating which counts for 3 hours total. Other than these 14 hours, a driver's 10 hours' sleep is mandatory. These rules are regularly observed by the digital log books installed in the truck and at corporate offices.

It is also important to point out when they are on a road or any interstate. The weigh station where each driver has options to have their truck and supplies weighed, they have what they call an "Easy Pass." When the drivers are driving from one state to another on the interstate, there are Welcoming centers at each Stateline for resting and eating for the truck drivers. Once a driver obtains an easy pass, it gives him the option to weigh his truck at the automatic self-weighing stations, drives his truck on the weigh station without any human guarding the area.

He has lights which give commands for the drivers to continue on to the interstate for the rest of the driving assignment or stop and park the truck at that weigh station. If the driver sees three greenlights blinking in order, then he is good to go. But if the driver sees three long red lights beeping that means he must park his truck in place at the truck stop to make the right required weight for what he is carrying in your truck.

Most of the weigh station on the highway remain open 24 hours a day on the interstate but some are closed. To help each other, drivers tell other drivers on the Citizen Band radio if a weigh station is opened or closed. If one hears the phrase "Open Sign Closed" it means the weigh station is closed and they can keep on driving without worrying about being weighed. On the matter of gas, there are two gas tanks per 18-wheeler, each can hold between 100 to 150 gallons of gas which can drive 1,000 miles per gas tank.

All of this and further involves Joe's truck driving skills and knowledge that he would require for transporting the UFO spaceship parts where they are needed. He seemed happy for taking the job. He knew that he would have to be careful while driving on the interstate, with rules and weigh stations. It reminded him of the wood that he had to brings to an undisclosed Military base for Rollins and Rollins. He had no clue where he went for this mission. It was like all of his driving and training experiences came down to this mission given.

While he was checking his tire weights and looking at the oil levels, a text that came in saying, "Starlings Island." He swapped the screen sideways looking at the pictures. After seeing the different angles of the island, he said, "Whoa!" The text read, "Virginia on the Chesapeake Bay." He was studying the maps to find a driving route, with the help of his partner, 'Bull Dog.' The text read on, "Island's spread between 75 to 95 acres of area." He had never delivered to an island before. More details started to pop up on his phone screen about the supplies, weights, time, delivery, maps and routes. The text ended with the initials D.E.B which meant Dr. Eugene Brooks

In Virginia Beach, Sundara was staring at the blueprints thinking, what was about to happen?! She thought to herself, if this plan works, my whole family can go home, to my planet and see everybody, Laura can look at where she was born. She liked Virginia, and she was in love with her husband Marc. They were a perfect match.

Marc walked in the living room to watch her staring at the UFO blueprints and she said, "You know Marc, we moved for the mission of water."

Marc replied with a question, as any reporter husband would, "The mission of water?"

She explained, "The planet knew that the water technologists were working on two projects here on earth. First project was to produce more drinkable water out of the sea by extracting the salt from the water and the second one was inventing new ways to use water for electricity, the latter being the major goal for those on earth.

Sundara, identified with the reports sent in from herself and others here on earth, "Planet Earth is known for water and life supporting atmosphere. All humans depend on water. We heard, on Earth they are making a drone that finds leaks in pipes underwater or above sea level, and helps in repairing them to save water for future communities. But my planet, Ooynt is not a water planet, just like another planet called Fiwusho, which also is waterless. We know there are many ocean planets.

However, we chose Earth because we knew about earth and humans. Also, that Earth is occupied with a good deal of salt water. The Earth's water has hydrogen inside. Our world is more advanced in this field. We just need the hydrogen from your waters to make a further advance system for us to go. I expect your ocean will be of the better use for you on earth honey. Your planet is great for you and all those who need it because you're the wateriest."

Marc replied, "Here on earth. water is used for many purposes, like cooking, for showers, drinking, putting out fires, swimming and growing food. There many more functions of water. It's very important here as well. Even for transportation across seas, water is very essential for our planet."

"Yes, we know this, honey. That's why we can't show up and withdraw all the water resources from Earth. It has to be done without a war and confused reactions. It must be done with other alternative solution. Marc dear, have you heard of Crystal Power Cells fuel?"

Marc was alarmed, he did not know what this was, as a reporter, he felt he knew about all the latest trends.

Honey, I want to say that your transportation objects fill up gas as a fuel, right?" Marc agreed with her. "With Crystal Power Cells fuel, you could drive your vehicles for 45 years or more... Can you imagine this, honey? Not worrying about buying gas every day. Crystal Power batteries would last forever."

"Whoa!" said Marc, "I couldn't imagine such a world! Maybe this is the fuel that we will have to find to power this spacecraft."

"We will certainly find out, one day."

Marc didn't take notes this time as her wife was giving him in all the information.

Sundara didn't want to talk about it anymore so to distract him she said, "Marc can you run to the grocery store? I needed more milk for dinner." Marc didn't want to go and wanted to hear more but he also was a good and caring husband so he answered, "Sure, I can."

While slowly walking out of the condo towards his jeep, he was thinking about what his wife was talking about. He had questions in is mind even while he was driving, all the way from home to driving on General Booth Boulevard and to the grocery store. He finally arrived at the store and wanted to park away from the store to have a decent parking spot. As soon as he got out of his jeep, behind him were two black trucks parked next to him, on both sides. Marc, tapped his cell phone to call his wife on speed dial but his phone went out before the call went through.

He turned around and looked at his passenger side door and there stood a figure, "Hello Mr. Dazet, we didn't mean to alarm you. We just wanted to see how you're doing."

Marc looked around the shopping parking lot to see for any possible help but it seemed like no one saw them and even if they did, they would have ignored in the fear of getting involved.

The figure kept talking, "We heard that…" then there was a pause, and Marc waited for the sentence to be completed. "… that you're going to have a visitor come down here from the northeastern coast. We think New Hampshire?" the figured turned to Marc for a response. Marc didn't agree or disagree he knew he had to use his brains.

"You can stay silence if you want. We know…"

Sundara called Marc many times but she found her phone going to the voice mail every time. She knew something was fishy. So, without wasting any time, she sent the Virginia Beach Local Police to the grocery store.

"Listen Marc, we hope the disturbance is not coming from a certain part of Virginia. Do you have anything else you want to tell us?"

Marc said nothing at all, he noticed the air in his jeep became a little thinner. "We know the lottery winner's coming here! It's kind of strange, don't you think?"

The figure now emphasized, "Think!" but he stopped as the police sirens could be heard in the background coming to the grocery store parking lot. Marc thought to himself I hope the police intervention doesn't aggravate the situation.

Then, his phone rang and he look down to see who it was before he could look up a again, and they were gone! He answered the call, "Marc! Marc! Honey Are you okay? Are you okay? You didn't answer your phone like you normally do…"

The Police sirens sent them right away. "Sundara, they surrounded me at the grocery store parking lot! OMG!".

The Police came looking for him. Three police cars came rushing to his jeep.

"I knew something was going on when you didn't pick your phone that's why I called them," said Sundara.

"I'm glad you did," said Marc.

The Police came from both side of his jeep. Both had their hands on the holsters, just in case something happens. Marc said in a loud voice, "I'm okay, Sir. I'm Okay!"

"Please step out of the vehicle very slowly," instructed the police officer. Marc followed the instructions. "Is everything okay, sir?"

Marc replied "Yes everything is okay."

Then they signaled and said something on their police radios, the lights from the other police mobiles now turned off. "Hello Mr. Dazet, what's going on? This is the second time we have been called to your car for help, did anyone visit you here?

Marc didn't tell them anything, he said, "Some dark trucks pulled next to my jeep as I was leaving my jeep to the store."

"Did they harm you, sir?"

"No, sir," he told the police.

"Do you want to press charges?"

"No, that's fine."

The police looked puzzled that why he didn't want to file charges. Marc was staring in a distance, as he was talking to the police. He did double take and he could see one of the black trucks park in a convenience store's parking lot.

"Okay Mr. Dazet, call us again if there is any trouble. Something must be going on in this place. It is the second time that this happened." The Police looked around his jeep to see if anything was fallen on the ground and they slowly vanished.

Marc couldn't go shopping after this, he put on his seat belt and his hands were shaking. Sundara was on the phone the whole time listening. He drove straight back home from the grocery store interrogation.

He made it home safely. Sundara stayed on the phone with him until she could see him walk in to the condo. Once the door opened, she ran and hugged him. Scared- Marc was still shaking, but he was also happy as he was safe after the incident.

Laura was in the other room and ran out when she heard the two talk. She could understand and use both Marc and Sundara's language, so she knew about the incident too. She was happy to see her Dad safe. She loved her parents very much. Being a half human and half Ooyntian. She cared about the safety of her parents, both her human dad and non-human mom.

Chapter 14

———◆◯◆———

There it was, in bold letters "Dairy Queen". They all gasped at the electronic sign in the air. "There you go Johnsons," Harold said proudly. "It's here. I told you, dad!" Zelda spoke excitedly from the back seat, "I can't believe it's here. They knew we all like Dairy Queen, maybe that's why it's here."

"Nope," Nolan responded, "Others like the ice cream with the fudge cover toppings too, Zelda."

They pulled in the area to see if the menu was different.

"I hope they have blizzards and banana splits this is all I'm craving at the moment," Hanna said in the background as their electric car pulled up with low sounds. When they parked the car, it seemed like they were the only one there. Harold walked to the ordering window and asked, "Hello, yes, I wanted to ask if I can place an order here?"

The people working there looked at Harold like from somewhere else. The staff member confused said, "No one does that here, coming here to place an order. We send them out usually…uh… and people orders from home… Umm…This is quite new for us, someone coming here and telling us what they want standing right here…"

"Can we place the order? I mean, is that okay?" asked Harold.

"Sure, please."

Harold waves his family to come to the window, and they all got out of the car and the crew working at Dairy Queen looked at them like they from another planet. At first, they didn't know what to do. When they all came to the window to place an order even people driving by that place drove slowly, thinking there must be something wrong there... As they were staring at the Johnson Family outside, one of the workers said, "I guess those people think we're getting robbed, Sir. This is a very odd scene..."

Hanna came to the window first excitedly and said, "Let the orders begin! I'll take a Blizzard, the one with Chocolate chip cookie dough." The worker took her order in amazement. The next was Zelda, "I'll take a Reese's Peanut Butter Cup Blizzard." Then Nolan stepped up and said, "I will have a Chocolate dipped ice cream cone. That it."

Then Harold said, "I want a Dairy Queen Banana Split." He thought they would not know what's in it, so he explained the recipe in the most exciting way. Harold spoke, "That's two banana halves made with, he held up three fingers, three scoops vanilla, one scoop chocolate and one strawberry... with chocolate, strawberry and pineapple sauces added with walnuts, whipped cream topped with a cherry.

They took his order and made it for them exactly as Harold wanted. With real people standing and waiting for their order it was different. They keep looking at them while making their orders. It didn't take them more than fifteen minutes, and they were done. Harold paid them, and they sat in the car and enjoyed their great discovery on this Military base yet. "It's just as good here at in Kansas, dad, just as good, maybe better," said Zelda. Cars were still driving by to see what was wrong. Zelda waved hi to them. It was a great experience for the whole family.

After their little outing, they went home. The night went by fast, bringing forth morning which began the second day on the base for the Johnsons. Harold had his sweat pants and pullover ready, and it had his name on them with Space Sahara 2.0 embroidered on the right side. He was getting ready for Physical Training this morning, PT they called it. He had done PT many times, but this was his first time on this base, and it was going to be different just like all other things.

Harold arrived at the field and saw his new friends Max and Bea. They were all shaking hands and greeting each other until Sergeant Backbone came out of nowhere, "Ten-Hut!" and everybody went into a line formation.

"Welcome back to PT everyone, Welcome back! I missed you guys. I want to remind everyone I'm the drill sergeant backbone. That's B.A.C.K.B.O.N.E. Then lowering his voice, he said, "We are happy that you're here and we have one purpose, that is to train you to be a 'Space Marine.' Now all of you were in different posts, from the Army, Navy, Marines, Air Force or Coast Guard but here you all are the same. So, step forward and do some Push-ups..."

Everyone stepped forward and did pushups. After a while Sergeant said, "Good! Now everyone up!"

Harold looked to his right and left and saw everyone had tired already.

"Okay, Stand up! I'm going to give you a piece of paper with some PT training. We took drills from all branches of military since all branches are represented here...I will read what's on the list. Follow me as I read, today we're going run half a mile, run as fast as you can!"

Everyone saw this on the list, and there a was letter (AFR) beside it. Number two read five pushups and carry two 30 pounds' canes sprinting. Then it said 3 miles run with a variety of obstacle courses. After the next objective, it stated (MRN). The sergeant kept reading, the third item on the list was to swim 300 meters/ 328 yards for good swim time. Next to the third one (NVY) was written. The last one was run 3 miles with the gear on. Learn performance nutrition, sports medicine, planted atmospheres. (ARY).... Now, you guys will have your PT once a week. And you have to accomplish the mentioned task for that week. You guys got that?

Everyone said, "Yes Sir!"

"Okay put the paper in your pocket, and let's start your run today! We're going to run half a mile as fast as you can. Now stand in the line, everyone! Stand in line! Let's go! Let's go! Let's go! They all did, and he said, "I will say 'backbone' three times and on the third time run like the wind."

The Sergeant was waiting for everyone to come up front. Then he looked around and said 'Backbone,' three times and they were off, running... There wasn't everyone first training. They knew what to do when they started to run. The trail took them around the dome and barracks it seemed. Harold saw soldiers passing by him briskly, and he was running ahead of two.

69

It was crazy many soldiers took this run to heart, boy did they run! The speakers on the side of the path telling them how far they ran, they had to run 880 yards. Some of them carried a pace. It had been a long time since most soldiers had to run this far. The next announcement said "300 yards completed. Five hundred eighty yards more in this run."

Zelda and Nolan were on lunch break, and they hardly knew anyone at the School. While they were eating, they noticed a girl wearing modern glasses and sitting by herself in the lunchroom complex. Nolan said to Zelda, "That's not cool. She is sitting alone. Let's go over there and sit next to her."

"No Nolan, we're new here. Let's not get into something we can't get out of."

"Come on, Zelda. let's go." Zelda agreed, and they went over to sit down. "Would you mind if we sit here? We're both new here and wanted to make new friends..."

The girl made the sign for No! to both, but Nolan ignored her and sat down, anyway.

"Hi, my name Nolan and this my sister Zelda how are you doing today? It's our second day here at the North Apex and our first time to be stationed on this base. What's your name?"

She looked up, paused and looked around the lunch complex at everyone, and she lifted both hands and the palms and told him, "My name is Renee Wiser. I would like guys to leave me alone."

Zelda and Nolan were stunned at her response... Nolan signaled her sister that they were staying. Renee was eating pears, and they were almost finished from the bamboo tray. And Nolan moved quickly I have an extra pear would you like mine?

She looked up and thought about what he said and then she said, "No I'm fine." Then Nolan stood up, and Zelda did too, and as they were walking away, Renee changed her mind, "Okay stay and I will take your pears for the exchange."

Nolan walked back, and Zelda followed. You know you made two new "Pears" of friends, and she laughed a little. Zelda asked, "Where are you from?"

Renee paused before answering "I'm from here."

Zelda didn't get that because in most bases many people were stationed from other bases. It was new for her to meet someone to say that they were from this base.

"Yes, I was adopted here, and I've been here ever since." Everyone was leaning in to hear more, but she remained quiet and didn't ask any questions, but she ate her pears and was wise not to say too much. It took a while for Renee to ask them where they were from, both said, "Fort Riley, Kansas. An Army base. She gave a puzzling look and said back "Where is that?"

Nolan paused, look around and asked, "You've never heard of Fort Riley? Okay, have you heard of the state called Kansas?"

She said, "Nope never heard of a place name Kansas, should I have?"

Zelda looked at her Brother and said, "Where are we? O my gosh! Where are we?

And the voice came from the cafeteria, saying that the lunch was over and to head back to classes. "Well, Zelda and Nolan from Kansas it was nice to meet you," Renee said.

Nolan shook her hand and said, "Nice to meet you too. We must talk again sometime. Is that okay?"

"If you have extra pear we can talk possibly again."

Everyone left at the same time to their section of the school.

Harold's legs were rubber from running the half-mile. He looked back to see others. Some soldiers were near him. He wasn't in the last place. He looked ahead and saw that Max was way ahead of him and thought, Boy, he can run! The speaker automation said, "You're at 750-yard marker, there are 130 yards left." The soldiers could hear Sergeant Backbone over the speaker cheering them, "Go! Go! Go! Let's Go! Run and finish. Let's Go Space Marines!"

It didn't seem that long, he saw other soldiers from a distance with water, and an electronic reader was taken the times as they came in one by one falling to the ground, many soldiers were on the ground, but some stood to lean over, all of them were huffing and panting by this first run. Harold too was in a superman pose but on the ground. Water came on him, and he felt great. He couldn't feel his legs. Others were coming in like airplanes landing on runway one at a time. Bea wasn't in the last place either. She came in like the rest of them, hugging the ground.

Hanna stayed at home for supporting her family, preparing food and making sure everything was perfect. She saw two buttons with strange words and pushed one of the buttons. There was a weird sound, but nothing happened. She thought, What's Andromeda and Triangulum?

Chapter 15

—◄( )►—

The shuttle pulled in from their ocean town to take the Brooks to the airport in Massachusetts. It was their first journey to mid-Atlantic Ocean. Brent had all the required paperwork as well as the Relic with him. He didn't trust anyone with his prized possessions when he was away from home especially after the incident. Margret and the Twins were happy for the weekend trip.

Before everyone jumped in the shuttle, there was a kind of a roll call. Margret was the head taking the roll call, "Jarvis, do you have your watch?"

"Yes, mom."

"Jared, did you check your wallet?"

"Checked."

"Honey, do you have your binoculars?" Brent brought some ATN BinoX-HD, a smart, day and night binoculars, top of the line for capturing the natural glimpses during the trip as it could take pictures and zoom up to many yards.

Brent teasingly asked her, "Did you bring your cheddar cheese brindles?"

She said, "Very funny Brent, you like them as much as I do. I hear you munching on them in your office all the time." This sweet sarcasm kept their relationship fun and alive.

She did not include Nelson on the roll call. He was more serious as he was their bodyguard. He spoke less and kept his eyes open at all times.

Portsmouth Airport was just at a fifteen-minute drive from Seabrook. They liked the helicopter ride better than traveling via cars and airplanes.

It was just their family traveling for the trip private and quick. They arrived at their hometown airport, and there was a sign near a hanger, "Charter Helicopters." Brent called out of the shuttle, "Mike, are you there? Mike?" Everyone jumped out of the shuttle and went into the office. Where's Mike? They all wondered and then saw a note written with a sharpie marker, it said, "Come around the back to 'The Brooks Family helipad.'"

They walked around the airplane hangar. Mike was waiting in the AgustaWestland AW139, he was already inside, pulling open a window, he asked, "It can accommodate eight people, will that be enough?"

The size and space of the helicopter amazed the family. Margret asked, "Eight people! What are you planning, Brent?"

"I can't tell you just yet," he replied in his new English accent.

They saw purple and white trim color paint, and it seemed longer than the helicopter they had last time while they flew to New Jersey. The door opened, and they brought their luggage onboard. It had plenty of room for them. Jared and Jarvis somewhat knew that the trip was about some land, but they didn't know it was about a whole island. After the Helicopter headphones were on, Mike spoke, "Welcome to Chatter Helicopters! Today we're flying to Yorktown, Virginia. We hope you will enjoy your stay and observe the beautiful scenery from New England's shores to the historic Yorktown, Virginia.

They were lifted in the sky like a hot-air balloon, without any noise. Everyone had headphones in their seats and felt great to be on a new adventure. Nelson was now a bit relaxed, being up in the air he knew where everyone was located, he felt at ease.

Mike spoke into the speaker, "I can't speak on what I know." Mr. Brooks told him to keep things on the hush-hush. Then, they pulled out of the coastal area and stayed primary on the East Coast. It would take about an hour and a half to two hours to reach Yorktown. The Helicopter costed more due to the comfortable leather seats which had drink holders and folded in different directions. Both Jarvis and Jared were lost in thoughts, wondering what would they see there. Margret seemed content. She liked to get out of New Hampshire every chance she had, and learn about other people and the history of the places.

Their ride was smooth, the Helicopter leaned to the left, and they all leaned left, maybe Mike wanted to feel the difference between this and their last helicopter in the air.

"What's that on the ground?" asked Jared.

Mike went low to show the family what was on the ground. It was the part of Long Island, New York.

"This is how Long Island looks from up here," Mike mentioned over the speaker.

Margret said, "It looks bigger than I expected. I thought Long Island was small."

Jarvis googled, "This is real! Wow! It has a population of over 7 million people. That's huge!" Brent said, "The Atlantic Ocean looked the same as Seabrook, I noticed."

They were moving closer to their destination, but it seemed like they were up there for just ten minutes. Jarvis being the quieter of the twins, it was the opposite in the air, Jarvis seemed to talk more. Jared was lost in the thoughts about the trip's purpose. Yorktown was only an hour away from Ocean City. Maryland shoreline was beautiful. Then, 35 minutes later, Brent instructed the pilot, "Okay Now!" and Mike immediately curved the chopper to the right.

"It seems like we went off a course of Yorktown," Mike replied, "We're getting close to the correct destination, Sir."

"Okay," Brent said all of a sudden, please fly lower so that we may see the ground closer."

To the family, he said, "Okay, I want you guys to see this. I have a surprise for everyone." They all paid attention. "Look to your right on the count of ten. Ready?" Brent said excitedly, "1, 2, 3, 4,5,6…7,8,9 and…10! Now we're at a section of the water called the Chesapeake Bay!" They all exchanged puzzled looks because they had seen plenty of ocean and islands on this trip and they were watching another island. Brent intoned, "It's called Starlings Island."

Jarvis and Jared still didn't get it. Brent kept going with the explanation for about 75 to 95 acres, and to his surprise, the family looked at him confused, trying to figure out the meaning of all the information. So, he decided to tell it more explicitly, "We now own Starlings Island!"

The family couldn't be more surprised. There was a pin drop silence for a moment, and they could only hear propellers over them. "Dad, could you please repeat what you just said?" The twins asked at the same time.

"Okay guys, look down." The Pilot just floated over the island. "We own this private island in Virginia." Everybody was so shocked that they understood it when Brent repeated it the second time, and then they burst into pure joy, "Yesses!" Jared said, "Yesses! we own an Island!" Jarvis High fived each other and Margret cried, "Do we really own it, honey?"

"Yes, we do, honey, we own this. That's why we're here," said Brent happily.

As they got closer to the island, they saw that some people were people there to greet them. It felt like they were on some TV shows like Fantasy Island, being greeted by Mr. Rourke and his tattoo, but this time it was for real. They looked around excitedly. They could not believe that the whole island was theirs.

Jarvis and Jared just sat down on the grass and looked around. Brent was excited he can now tell his family this was the pent-up secret that he had been holding for a long time.

"We can build an amusement park here or have a small town here on the island. There is a lot that we can do here. We will still have our home in New Hampshire, but we have an Island too." Margret just ran with no care in the world, as fast she could, yelling at the top of her lungs, "Mine! It's all mine! Our family owns an Island, Honey!" then she sprinted back and jumped into Brent's arms.

Nelson was speechless too, "Mr. Brooks you own this?"

"Yes, we do, Nelson. Our family can now build here."

"Mr. Brooks, there's a lot to learn about this island."

"Learning as we go will be our keep. We will bring in others to help

us build. I talked with Mr. Atushi and asked if he would like a Dojo gym here, and, he was happy about this idea and training you guys." Jared and Jarvis liked the idea too.

Brent told everyone that they were coming back tomorrow with some friends who live here, Marc and his family, "That is why I asked Mike to get a bigger Helicopter for us this time. Let's all head to Yorktown to put our luggage away, and we'll meet my friend tomorrow."

They all agreed. Mike started the luxury helicopter from their journey from Starlings Island to Yorktown, and everyone hopped in. Having an entire island to their name, the Brooks family had a different feeling that they were a part of something new and big.

In Seabrook, Yautja looked at her map on the wall which had everything she needed. Trying to study how her plan would work, she looked at the whole map with streets and buildings there were airports in Portsmouth and the dots that went to the Brooks residence in Seabrook. There were dates, time and even seconds.

Over and over she went through the plan that she had put together. Yautja was almost ready. On her map, she had various holographic pictures, an image of the flying helicopter calculating its pace. The description under each image was in a language that humans would never understand. It seemed to show many shapes, and it contained many sounds effects as well. It was like the map was telling Yautja what to do.

The Map mentioned the important days regarding the trip to be Friday, Saturday and Sunday. She thought about the timing and also about the bodyguard, she had this in mind that she didn't have much history and whereabouts of the bodyguard.

Chapter 16

---◄)►---

Marc looked for his digital camera, something that is all reporters' must have. Sundara made sure that she had everything in place for they were about to meet her husband's new friend.

"Wow Marc, we are meeting a lottery winner from New Hampshire tomorrow. She always liked to hear the newspaper stories from her husband and other reporters who worked with him. She had learned a lot about this community and the Earth. Where she was from, they had the newspapers named 'Anoint.' There was plenty of news on it. Since she was raised around the faction of travelers who traveled to other planets, Anoint contained news from many other languages too. She had studied various languages of Earth too.

"We have a newspaper which tells about different places and planets too, as you have yours on Thursdays'. A lot is going on outside, world even in our own surroundings," said Sundara.

"What time is Mr. Brooks picking us up?" Sundara asked Marc.

"I don't know honey, but I will receive a phone call with update today." After a while, his phone rang, and it was Brent, "I'm in Virginia, Marc. We made it."

"Great! I'm glad you came to see my state. How was the trip?"

"It was great. We're in Yorktown."

Marc wondered why didn't they stay in Virginia Beach? The ocean resort area is famous all over the globe, "I can't believe you're here in Virginia I'm going pinch myself."

He took the cell phone from his ear and covered the speaker with his hands and told Sundara that the Brooks had arrived. She smiled back and picked up some conversation.

"Can we meet tomorrow in the afternoon?"

"Yes," Marc said, "We will drive to Yorktown and meet you there. It's been a while since we saw that historic area.

"Yes, see you tomorrow around 3 to 5 pm. Is that fine, Marc?

"Yes, that would be great." Then Marc looked at Sundara and thought, should we tell them about the Blueprints, honey? she said, "Not yet, we don't even know how we're going to do this."

Laura was home, and she knew she wasn't going too far from Virginia Beach. She liked traveling just like her Mom. She wondered where would they go tomorrow, and asked her mom, "Mom, where are we going?"

"We're going to Yorktown, sweetie."

"Nice," Laura was happy for the upcoming short trip.

Although it wasn't going to be a long trip still, she was still happy for this road trip. Next morning, the Jeep was ready and packed. Marc decided to bring the blueprints with him just in case. He kept them in a safe place in the Jeep, Sundara was ready, she wore a trendy sweater with space look. It had stars and moons on it. And Marc wore a Cal Poly Mustangs college visor hat and brought his music for the trip. It was an hour's drive from Virginia Beach. Sundara didn't know everything about Virginia, so she asked, "Honey tell me about Yorktown."

Now on the road, heading on I-65 West, North of the oceanfront. The scenery was always great during this season, with lush green trees and gentle breeze.

"Well honey, Yorktown is of great historical importance for us. It is the place where the Revolutionary War of 1781 took place. You would find many museums there too.

Laura was glad where ever she was going, she had a baseball hat on and was listening songs on her smartphone but not too loud just in case her parents want to talk to her.

"Williamsburg is just as historical as Yorktown honey," Marc told Sundara.

Then he called Brent on the phone to tell him he's on the way and Brent was happy and ready for meeting him. It didn't take too long before they arrived Yorktown. It was a relaxing one-hour drive. When they entered Yorktown, they saw a brick sign that said 'Historic Yorktown 1691' there was a welcome center for tourists to tour while they drove into the area.

Marc said to his wife, "We're looking for a Bed and Breakfast called Marl Inn Bed and Breakfast, honey." Sundara was looking on the GPS in the Jeep, and she had to ask Marc what was a Bed and Breakfast, he was used to Sundara's such questions about life on earth. He was patient as he knew he would be doing the same when they travel to her home, Ooynt.

"Well, it's a place where they make breakfast for you while you stay there. They offer many rooms like a hotel, but it's in a home comprising of five to six rooms, and they have a quaint style, honey. You would like it a lot. There are many such places in this area."

She looked it up on their phone and passed the pictures to Laura. It was new to her. It was on Church Street in Yorktown. Marc forgot how cool it was to see something different from what they usually see. Sundara called the bed-and-breakfast, and a voice came on and said, "Hello, can I help you?"

"Yes, we have reservations, and we are arriving there soon."

"Sure! My name is Amy, Welcome to Marl Inn Bed and Breakfast. Can't wait to see you."

"Yes, we can't wait to get there. See you soon."

"Great. See you soon."

Sundara gave Marc two thumbs ups in the Jeep as they kept going.

The Brooks family couldn't contain themselves about what just happened to them yesterday on the Chesapeake's Bay. They were still shocked after discovering that they own a whole island. Everyone was busy thinking about what they wanted to build on the island. Both Jared and Jarvis were bouncing idea's back and forth. Jarvis said, "How about having a secret water slide in our closets which opens in a pool?" Both giggled at the idea.

A lot of greenery surrounded the bed-and-breakfast, and outdoor furniture and plants were well-maintained just as well as the indoor ones. They were in their rooms. "Wow, we didn't know this was quite near, and we waited for our friends from New Hampshire come here to make plans for this place," said Marc.

They were relaxing when a knock on the door. It was Brent, "Hey, welcome to the bed-and-breakfast, I am so glad that you are here. We're not too far from your room here. I want to show you something when you have the time. I was thinking, after lunch, we can all see this surprise. Would that work for you all?"

"Sure, after lunch seems great."

Sundara came in the room thinking would he recognize that I'm not from earth? He looked, paused and reached out his hand to her. She said, "I'm Sundara. How are you doing, Mr. Brooks?"

"I'm very well. Thank you."

"Nice to meet you for a change. You're the Lottery winner from New Hampshire, yes?

"Yes, your husband wrote a story on me in New Hampshire. He did a good job on the story."

Then Laura came from around the corner. She was shy and didn't say much. Watching her enter so quietly Brent said, "And whom might this be?"

"This is our daughter, Laura," Marc introduced. She reached out her right arm to say Hi.

"Hi there," replied Brent, "It was nice to meet you guys. You will meet my twins and wife soon at lunch. I'm going to get out of your hair now. See you downstairs, Okay?

"Okay," they all agreed. Brent walked out of the suite and Sundara thought you think he saw in me. "Nope," Marc said, "Many people do not see except if they are around you for over two days."

The Brooks were unpacking in the room for their weekend trip. Brent walked back to his room, checked the paperwork and Relic and everyone was buzzing about their plans for the new island and things they all wanted to do. Brent said, "Guys, don't tell the Dazets about the island in the Helicopter. I want this to be a surprise for them." Everybody agreed.

They all came down starts within two hours, ready to meet the brooks. There was a shuttle outside the bed-and-breakfast with a sign on the door, which said, "Open the door Dazet family!" Knowing it was for them, Marc opened the shuttle door, and the driver greeted them, "Welcome! Come on in. I'm your driver for this trip with the Brooks."

They all hopped in. The Brook family was nowhere in sight. Something confused them on what was going on there. They went along with the plan, anyway. Then the driver started their ride.

"Do you know where the Brook family went?" Marc asked the driver.

The Driver replied, "They're already waiting for you."

"Can you tell where are going exactly?"

"Yes, sir. Hoffman's Farm Airport."

And they drove down the road, there was a Helicopter, and they could see Brent waving at them standing by it. The driver dropped them there.

"Hi there, Welcome and come on in, have you been in a Helicopter before?"

Marc as a reporter has been in many rides, but his daughter there had her first ride today. Sundara was not new to air travel.

"Yes, let's all go! We're ready."

"Welcome aboard, Dazet family."

Mike started the luxury ride, and everyone stood back a little while the propellers rotated in circles, then from the steps, everyone jumped in.

There was plenty of room for everyone. Everyone put on the talking sets, and the twins introduced themselves, "Hi, I'm Jarvis, and I'm Jared," as they shook hands with them. Laura introduced herself to the twins as well. When everybody settled down, Marc asked Brent, "So, where we are going?"

Chapter 17

———◦◦◦———

Mike made an announcement in the helicopter on the microphone. He told everyone to stay in their seats and to make sure their seatbelts are fastened. "One more thing guys, if you want to talk just push the green button and it will let you talk, to everyone here will be able to hear you." Laura pushed the button to test it out, "Hello, Hello," and everyone waved at her "We hear you."

Then they were lifted in the air and the journey towards the waters started. Brent kept talking. He was happy that they all were down for this fantastic experience. Sundara looked outside, being close to the sky and moving at the same time was a nice feeling. Their ride took off steadily, then soon they were in the air and could see land surrounded by water.

After a while, Brent said, "There it is!"

Something confused Marc just as it puzzled the Brook family, "What is it?"

"Look, right there! Did you see?" said Brent excitedly.

Marc kept looking, and said, "It's just another island."

"It is not just any island, my friend. It's our family island. I bought it for our family. This was the total surprise."

Both Sandra and Marc turned towards each other and froze. They both were thinking the same thing at the same time. Brent kept talking, "Yes, it's called Starlings Island. It is about 75 acres of land with water surrounding it".

Everyone was very glad. Margret and twins had seen the island earlier, but they still had the same delighted feelings as if they were seeing it for the first time. Mike circled the island so that everyone could have a closer look at it. Then he picked a spot to land and turned off the engine, and everyone was waiting to get out and roam on the island.

Brent was the first one out. As his feet touched the ground, he said, "We will keep the name 'Starlings Island', it fits quite well." Then, Margret jumped out and pointed to an area and said, "Over there will be our atrium," like it was a house, "And I haven't decided what I want over there yet," she said pointing towards an open area, "That's all I have so far. Honey, you wanted a Dojo for Mr. Atushi, yes?"

"Yes, honey," replied Brent.

Marc couldn't contain himself. He took his wife and went for a walk a little away from the Brooks. They walked maybe 30 steps away from them. "Honey," Sundara said, "Are you thinking what I'm thinking?"

Marc said nothing but made an agreeing gesture.

Sundara was thrilled, "Oh my gosh! How in the world did this happen? Everything fits. There's enough area to build the spaceship from the blueprints, honey! I'm not sure how are we going to tell them this."

"You know Sundara, Dr. Brooks told me that I would meet others who will help me in this, and he was not kidding. I never thought he was talking about his own nephew!"

Both were awestruck, looking in the sand. There were enough water and land to make the plan work here. Laura looked over and tried to read their lips to know what they were saying. She seemed to pick up their conversation easily. Laura thought everyone could hear conversations. This gift to listen from far away was new to her. She also knew how to change the temperature so this ability of good hearing was an addition to her skill set.

Brent called, "Is everything okay over there?"

"Yes," Marc said as he walked back to everyone. Laura stared at them as they were walking back. She knew what they were talking about but didn't show it. She kept staring at her parents and the island.

85

Jarvis and Jared ran to them, "Do you like the island?

The Dazets said, "Yes, a lot."

Marc said to Brent, "Do you remember the show, The Gilligan's Island?"

"Yes, I do."

"What happened on Gilligan's Island, Dad?" Jared asked.

"Well, it was a TV show in the 80s that we all grew up with. It came on around 5 pm on the weekdays. What happened was that a two-person crew of charter boat SS Minnows had five passengers. They were off to a two-hour tour, but they get ship-wrecked to a Pacific island."

Margret said, "Yep, your right."

"Yes," Marc keeps talking there were Gilligan, the Skipper, and Thurston Howell III who was the millionaire stuck with them. The cast also had Ginger Grant-the movie star, the Professor, and Mary Ann. It was a great show, funny and smart."

"We're like Gilligan's Island, only this island called Starlings Island," Jared added.

And everyone started laughing at Jared's comment.

"This is a different location, okay? You are free to walk around," said Brent, "Also, if you guys want to add to the island feel free to suggest, we have a lot of land here to build something great for us and others." Both Marc and Sundara held their speech for a good reason.

Watching them so quiet Brent said, "You can leave if you like, my pilot can take you back to the bed-and-breakfast."

Marc. "We like it out here, and I know you want to explore on your own Mr. Brooks. We're just happy you brought this island." Marc said looking at Sundara. They both smiled.

Laura was happy to meet Jared and Jarvis. The whole concept of identical twins was new to her. However, it connected her with them as Laura was different but so were, they. The twins didn't know she was different. But Laura felt safe with them as new friends. Nelson watched everyone and made sure everyone was safe. In his view, having a more remote place secured the family. He liked his new project.

Sundara didn't want to stay to much longer. She was always in fear that everyone would know who she was and someone would notice that she was not from Earth. So, she hesitantly asked if they could come back again. Marc knew what she was talking about and understood. Brent said, "Sure I will tell Mike to start the Helicopter. I think we all are going to come back later." It took about fifteen minutes, and everyone was back in their seats.

Margret was still doing the island's interior designing in her mind. She didn't let it stop even on the helicopter. She was thinking about the Indian Tribe in New Jersey and how she could dedicate something from the tribe to the island. Everyone had their own ideas and plans about the Island in the helicopter.

Even the pilot thought, how great it would be neat if they had a runway here and a mini airport. It didn't take much long before they were back at the Marl Inn. Marc and Sundara opened their door with Laura not too far behind. As soon as the door closed behind them, there was a burst of Joy hugging and yelling, running around the room, Laura thought something good has happened. Both knew this was their fate to build the spaceship on Starlings island. They knew it.

Marc thought, Dr. Brooks was right! He told me that people would come in and share information to help and it happened just like that. But how will we get the material and the large machine parts transported to the island? How would he tell Brent about his family and how would he react about Sundara and Laura?

Sundara having read his mind was thinking the same thing. Their joy was transformed into careful thinking as to how were things going to happen. Laura, on the other hand, was enjoying the trip a lot she said to Sundara, "I like the twins. They are cool. I have never had friends who look the same. I can't tell one from the other.

Impulsively walking out of the room, Marc called Dr. Brooks, he recalled how to call on Dr. Brook's cell phone, it's February that's 02, the day 17th and then the year 2019 so the number is 02-17-2019 and waited for the phone to ring.

"Hello Dr. Brook, it's me Marc, the reporter." The call was answered, Marc listened intently, trying to comprehend if the voice was from the past or the future. He wasn't sure that he would hear Dr. Brook's voice again, but he knew that Dr. was somewhere.

"Dr. Brook, I wanted to update you on something. Your nephew has done it. You told me there were going to be people, and things would happen on their own. You were right!"

"Yes, Marc. Everything I said is true, but what has happened there?"

"Well, Brent has bought an island in Virginia." Dr. Brook's ears perked up, *"He did?"*

"Yes, it is big, and it is the right size to build what's on the blueprints."

Dr. Brook paused, Marc thought the call had disconnected, so he asked, "Hello, are you there?"

"Hello, Yes, I'm here, I was just thinking. Could you tell me the name of the island that he bought?"

"Yes, it's called Starlings Island, right off the coast of the Chesapeake Bay. It's divinely beautiful."

Just then, he heard a voice in the background, "The invisible blanket has to be tested more, Eugene. Before it goes out, it must be!" Dr. Brooks covered the phone with his hand and started talking to someone. Marc could hear the muffled conversation but couldn't make out the exact words. Then he got back to the phone, "Marc, this is it. The time is approaching as I mentioned, you see?"

"Yes," he kept going on, *"How are we going to tell Brent about the blueprints?"*

"You will not have to tell him. Time will reveal everything. You just have to stay near him and remember that other people will be helping. Keep an open mind okay. Also, call me back if you have any more updates and thank you for the call."

"Okay, Dr. Brooks. Take care."

"You too, and call me anytime of the day or night."

Marc wanted to stay on, to hear if there were any sounds or information regarding where Dr. Brook's current location. But the phone clicked, and Marc just stood there looking into the silent Yorktown.

Chapter 18

——•◦•——

Colonel Mathews was at his desk looking over updates with Harold and his training so far. He thought it was too early to have an assessment of progress. The colonel looked at his running and the finishing times and thought that Harold was doing well for it was his third day. He turned on a special LED light which seemed to control more than just lighting in the room, on the side of its panel it said, "Life Operation Space Sahara." He tapped a button, and a screen came up from his desk, and it was a kind of caller interface.

On the screen, a person named 'Space bravo Backwards Commander Jorge Coleman' appeared. Colonel greeted him, "Hello Sir, how are you doing?"

Commander Jorge saluted the Colonel and said, "I'm doing fine, Colonel. It is the first day of training here, so I wanted to see if everything was okay here. Take it easy on them. It's their first day."

I will Sir. Then the screen went down, and the LED light turned off by itself.

Before heading out for the third day of training, Harold was drinking his morning coffee. Before heading out for his third day of training, he walked into the children 's room and saw them sleeping, so he went back to talk to Hanna, "Dear, how are you doing so far here?"

"I am doing okay, just taking some time getting used to no plastic items. It's like I have to train my mind for this process. The toothbrushes are different, so are the cups. Even the way they bake and package food is different, honey. I like it, but it takes some time to get used to this stuff.

Then, there's a mysterious button in the living room with names that I have never heard of. Things are pretty different here.

However, our children do seem to like their new school. I don't think it would take much long for them to get used to the school. But I feel stuck, kind of like the board game we used to play, 'Sorry game,' the only difference is that all of you are moving on the board but I'm stuck on the home base."

"It's Ok honey I'm glad this base is very advanced. Anyways, I will call you later today to check up on you." Hanna smiled and said, "Thank you, honey, for taking us to Dairy Queen. Did you see their faces when we told them we wanted to order in person? All the workers were in shock. I loved it! And the ice cream was good too."

"Yes!" Harold joined in, "The banana split was so good that I ate mine slow on purpose, that's why I was the last to finish." They both laughed, and he could see her eyes reflecting the happiness. Watching her laugh was like falling in love with her all over again.

After hugging his wife and having said the sweet goodbyes, Harold went to work. He was supposed to look up a building that said, "Space bravo Backwards" He went around the base but couldn't see anything. Even driving around the base again didn't help, but then, he noticed something. All the domes were facing the road, but one seemed to face the other way. He looked at it carefully, did a double-check and yes, they had built the building different from all other. Even the parking lot was different.

Cars were permitted only if they drove backwards. He saw cars going there backwards instead of forward, it was weird. So, Harold turned his car backward and drove in. After showing the fingerprint and gate went down into the ground for me allowing me to go in but backwards.

He even parked his car that way. As he was getting out of his car, he saw soldiers going in the building walking backwards. It was very unusual. Harold went to the door to scan his ID, but the scanner seemed to be installed in a lower position in the dome entrance. After some time, he figured out that he had to turn around and use his hands behind his back to get identified, that's why it was in a lower position.

So, he turned around and took his right palm and held it down on the screen. When the door opened, he too walked in backwards. It was very hard for him to remember that he had to walk opposing to the forward position, but he seemed to forget that he must walk backward. As he is walking down the hall, he saw that even the pictures were displayed according to the walking style.

Finally, he saw a sign written in backward that said "emocleW of ovarbecapS sdrwkcaB." He just sat there reading the sign for a few minutes, thinking what does this unit do? Soldiers also reverse-saluted him. So, did he, it was my first time doing this.

He went into a room, and again there were chairs in the opposite direction. Some people knew what to do, and others new like myself followed them. It was different to train the mind this way.

Then, the commander came into the room, and he said, "Welcome!" his back was facing us, and we could see his face on the screen. He said. "I want to welcome everyone on the first day of the training." Then, he told us to stand, and he shook all the New soldiers' hands. He approached us in a way where all of us were standing in reverse and were able to shake hands.

He went back to the front and kept speaking, "Here at Space bravo 'BW' you will learn and train in reverse. It will be difficult for you all for about weeks, but with the time you will get the hang of it. It will be harder for you to catch on to this training, I know. But once you're done, you'll be an expert and will know the tactics. I can't tell you all in this manner about what we have to learn in this division. There are planets in our solar system that go in the reverse position."

Everyone looked at each in shock.

"Yes," he continued, "Earth moves forward, and so does time proceed forward on earth. However, we must prepare you for anything that's out there. I will show you something. Please step in this door." It was an area in the dome training room. Everyone went in one person at a time. Harold waited in the line until it was his turn.

The Commander instructed Harold, "Please walk in backwards and do not be alarmed." He turned around to walk into this area, and the door slammed shut. Then, he noticed something. Harold was right-hander, and, in this room, it was his left hand that became strong, and his right hand became the weaker hand.

He tried to punch the air with his right hand to make sure this was true. Everything was in revered motion. Then a voice spoke, "Welcome to the Reverse Speech Model." In this room, the words came on a scene, and Harold had to speak the words, but when he spoke, the words sounded different. On the Screen it said 'Car,' but its sound came "Rac." Another word flashed on the screen, "House" he spoke the word, and it came out to be 'Esuoh.'

The voice told him to just talk in a usual way, so he said something Radom this time, "This is great! How on Earth can this be done?" and every word in this separate area in the dome came out foreign. There was a timer on the door, and he had one more minute in this area, so Harold said the names of everyday things and each word came out different, it was very new to him.

After his time was over the door opened automatically, and he came out backwards of course. The other soldiers who had been through the same process didn't speak much, and they were only amazed at the diversity. Harold went over to them and said: "Can you believe what just happened in there?"

One soldier said, "Have you heard of the word 'Pareidolia'?"

"No, I have not heard of this word."

"Please look it up when you're at home. It's something to do with a perceived pattern," he said after watching something that they had never seen before they felt amazed like kids. Harold went over to sit down, waiting for others to complete this process.

Zelda and Nolan at school were ready in their sections for their classes. It was their first day after the orientation.

The students sat at their desks, and the teacher arrived. The instructor turned to a screen on the wall and said, "Hello everyone, Welcome to your first day at class." It seemed like everyone knew each other, only a few faces were new. Every desk had a button, and the teacher asked them to tap it, and this opened a TC computer, a tiny computer.

In the desk, she saw a computer, and it looked like a mini computer it was so small one could fit it in the back pocket. This little item was programmed to do everything. The notes and textbooks were inside this computer for this class, and when they went for the next class, the books for that class were added automatically to the device.

Zelda looked at and thought it was tiny. Wow! She thought, how do I type on this?

She kept talking pushing the button, and the screen showed a typing board in a hologram in the air. She started using the keyboard pad in the air. It was an evolutionary change for them.

Her bother was going through the same learning curve in his class. Nolan's teacher explained to him about the TC computers, "These are made of bamboo and metal. You can take it home and even if you're going somewhere, and you can use it on the go." No one raised their hands while the teacher was talking.

"Students, you have an AI friend with each TC."

Nolan thought what an AI buddy is? he could not understand anything, "Can you please explain what's an AI buddy?"

The teacher said, "Of course, AI means artificial intelligence. Please click on the AI tab on your TC." He did, and there it was. A person's voice came on which sounded like someone of his age, "Hi Nolan, my name is Hinge."

He was surprised, "Hi Hinge."

"It's nice to meet you. I will be your AI buddy. Anytime you need something. I'm right here."

Zelda's friend was "Mime." She was glad to have a new friend. The Teacher said, "Wherever you go in life, they will be there to help you while you're in school or out. It's a gift from North Apex High School."

Chapter 19

———————×( )×———————

Marc and Sundara enjoyed their stay at Yorktown. They revisited the Starlings island with the Brooks before they headed back home. The Brook family had a notepad and designs for the island throughout their two-day stay. Now, it was time to head back to New Hampshire to put those plans into action.

"Marc, thanks for coming and joining us. I hoped you liked the surprise," Brent said to Marc and Sundara standing beside their car before they left.

"Yes, it was a great trip."

"It was very new for us too, Marc. Well, do write your ideas about the island and we'll add them to the island plans."

Both shook hands.

"We will talk again, Marc."

"Yes, sure." With this, everyone wished each other a safe trip. Laura said goodbye to the twins and Margret was glad to meet everyone, and so was Sundara. The Jeep drove off to the interstate back to the oceanfront.

Preparing the Helicopter for the Brook family, Mike checked the back revelers and filled up the gas with 'Jet-A'. Around noon, the Brooks took off and were ready to head back.

Brent looked around to check everyone's seatbelts to make sure a safe ride back home. Their journey was quick and easy. As they reached Seabrook, Mike spoke in the headset, "And here we go back to another part of the Atlantic Ocean that is Seabrook, New Hampshire."

The trip back home was quicker than the one to Virginia, back then, everyone knew why they were going there, but on the way back home, their thoughts were stuck on Starlings Island. They felt like it was a one-hour trip back home while it took two hours to land on the Portsmouth Airport. As they landed, their shuttle was waiting for them.

Nelson jumped off first and opened the door of the shuttle, then came the family. They were all in the shuttle and Mike put the helicopter back in the hanger. Jarvis was telling Jared "What a trip! Did you get the notepad with all of the notes?" Jarvis asked.

"No, I forgot them on the helicopter. Stop the shuttle! One second please," Jared said, "I'm going to get the notepad."

The shuttle stopped, Jared jumped out and ran to the hanger where Mike parked the jet. He called out, "Mike are you there? Mike?" There was no answer. Then all of a sudden, Jared turned around and looked up. He knew something was wrong.

He tried to move his feet but he couldn't, he said, "Hey, what's going on here?"

Yautja came from the inside the Hanger grabbed him. Jared walked with her as he couldn't fight her. She walked into a hole in a fence of the airport, and they both went through that hole. On the other side of the hole, her muscle car was parked. She opened the door, and made Jared sit in the back seat, then she drove off somewhere.

The shuttle was waiting for Jared with its engine running. Five minutes turned in 10 minutes and about 30 minutes were passed when Brent told the driver to go back to the Hanger, "Make it quick!" Brent said.

Nelson was thinking Oh my gosh! What happened to Jared? I should have gone back with him. When they approached the hanger where Mike was supposed to be, Nelson "Oh my gosh, no way! No way!

All of them hastily jumped out of the van, before it even stopped properly. Nelson ran the fastest of all and opened the Hanger door. Jared was gone.

He was nowhere. Everyone kept calling his name. But there was no answer. Margret and Jarvis were reduced to tears after they found no trace of Jared. Brent went looking for his son in every nook and cranny of the hanger. Brent called Mike, but his phone was repeatedly going to the voicemail. They were anxious.

It was hours before they got back in the shuttle. Nelson rode with them. He was upset about what had happened on his watch. The feeling that he let everyone down broke him and at the same time it made him determined to find the one who did this to the family.

The gate opened to their home. Everyone was upset. Jarvis fell silent not knowing what to do without his brother. The security gate opened, and it took a long time to reach home from the secret entrance. All of them went inside perplexed.

Around 11 pm, Brent got a call from an unknown number. He picked up, suspecting it to be the ransom call. "Hello, who is this? Jared is that you!?"

There was a pause, and Brent was roaring at the phone, "Who is this!?" Then Yautja's voice came over the phone, "Hello. Mr. Brent Brooks."

Brent didn't know this voice.

"You don't know me, but I know you. There is something you have that I need." Brent was now sure that it's about Jared, "Hey, give me my son back! Who is this? I want my son back!" The whole family came to the living room after hearing Brent on the phone call.

Yautja went on, "You have a Relic, and I would like to trade your son Jared for the Relic." In his fluster, Brent didn't quite understand what she said, "Can you say again?"

Yautja repeated it, a bit louder this time "You have a Relic. I want you to trade it in exchange for your son Jared."

This time Brent heard every word that she said. He felt guilty for having the relic because of which something terrible could happen to his son. "I will do it. When and where can we do this?" "I will call you back with the instructions tomorrow." Brent said quickly, "No. No. Not tomorrow. Today! This very minute! Let's trade right now." But the phone went to the dial tone.

Brent looked to his family in shock, as the phone ended, "Some lady called me to trade the Relic for Jared." Margret felt a panicked, "Oh my good God!" She went into a room away from everyone to look for some local detective. She searched and found one. He called the number, and the person answered, "Detective Thomas Reilly here. How may I help you?"

Maggie tried to contain her the best she could, "Someone has kidnapped my son, and I need your help. Can you get here as soon as possible?" The detective said, "Yes, give me your address, and I'll be there within an hour. Is that Okay?"

"Yes, please," Margret hung up the phone. She informed Brent about the detective. Everyone was in shock but relieved that a detective was coming over to help them. Brent checked the Relic, making sure it was safe. Almost an hour later, there was a buzz on their intercom, Brent went to the monitor area and saw there was a person in a Ford Mustang Shelby 1965 GT 350.

He beeped, and the person said, "I'm Detective Reilly. I'm here to see your family about a case." Margret heard the voice and recognized that it was the same voice over the phone. Brent let him in, a medium height man came out wearing a long trench coat, and it seemed as if he had a limp. He rang the doorbell, and Nelson answered the door, "Yes, may I help you?

"Yes, My name Detective Thomas Reilly. I'm here to see the family."

"Yes, please come in." The whole family was waiting for him to come. Margret greeted him and said dolefully, "Hello, my son has been kidnapped, please help us find him."

Jarvis was looking at the Detective and didn't say much. The detective pulled out a notepad and asked everyone to sit down. He would like to ask some questions and start the investigation right away. Everyone gathered in the living room, he pulled up a chair and sat in front.

The Brooks were vexed, sitting in complete disbelief. Brent told what happened at the hangar and then he discussed the mysterious phone call, "I got a call from someone, they want something I have in exchange for my son."

The detective made notes and asked, "What was that they wanted? Can I see this item?"

"Yes," Brent brought him to the office and showed him the Relic, "This what they want."

Detective Reilly took a picture of the item, "I have never seen such item before, where did you get it from? If I may ask."

Brent said, "I got it from a trip to Wanaque Reservoir, New Jersey. A native American chief gave me this Relic."

"I see," said the detective, "I wonder why the kidnapper wants this item instead of money, for the exchange of your son? It must be vital.

Brent took him back in the living room. "Wait, wait, aren't you the guy who won the lottery a little while back?"

"Yes, I am that person."

"Yes, I saw on TV, he said adding this in his notes writing Reporting Party, and they headed to the Hangar. The detective said, "It is best we start working this case now, the first four hours are crucial for solving the case."

"Tell me about Jared, everyone can talk one at a time, and I will take down some notes."

Jarvis said, "We're twins. They took my brother."

"Did he have any enemies?"

"No."

"Was he in a gang or anything?"

"Everyone shook their head in denial."

"Did he have any mental or emotional outbursts?"

"No, nothing of that sort but he sure is outspoken and louder than Jarvis," said Margret. Jarvis also described his brother whom he knew the most." The detective wrote outspoken. Active person.

"Any drug uses?"

"No," Margret said, "If there were anything like that, I would have known about this."

"Where did the kidnapping take place?"

Nelson said, "At Hanger C, Portsmouth Airport in town about two hours ago."

The Detective texted someone in another department to send a team to the Portsmouth Airport, "I'm sending the evidence team there. They will have to pick up evidence and research all the activity that area on what happened 24 hours before and after your son went missing." The Team was dispatched out for the field interrogation.

"Most of the crimes like this show evidence on the scene. Sometimes the criminal leaves their hair or something that else regarding the crime which becomes our clue. We will look into the neighborhood as well, know who lives around here and also the drifters".

"Do you guys know any of your Neighbors?"

Margret said, "No, we know no one here we've kept to our self for security purposes."

"According to the standard procedures, most Detectives rope off the area and put the phones on trace. Same will happen in this case. I know it is hard for everyone here today but you all have to be strong. I will explain you everything about what we're doing to find the culprit. In the meanwhile, can I browse your call log to see if I can get the number and information about the person called you?"

"Yes," Brent said, "She sounded like a lady. And she was calling from a faraway location." The detective wrote in his notepad while scanning his cell phone for a number. "I think it's better not to put this in the news, this might alert the kidnapper, and this won't help with the case."

"Thanks, detective, we want the same. We will tell no one."

"I'm going to trace your cell for the upcoming phone calls, Brent. This lady will call again on this number and then we can track down where she is from."

"Yes, that would be fine," said Brent.

She is going to call back as she said. As soon as she calls, Nelson, you have to call me on your phone, and we will trace the call. Now, I must go back to the office and talk to my data team as we put the pieces of this puzzle together. Hold on to The Relic, when you meet her, we will be there too." With that, he told everyone we are going to solve this case and get Jared back.

Margret said, "Okay." She was still upset and didn't say much, but she was glad for calling him in to investigate. While the detective was walking toward the door, Jarvis came to him and said, "Please find my brother. I'm not sure how I can handle things with him gone. We are inseparable. It's important that we find him."

"I'm here to provide whatever help you need to find Jared. Don't worry, Jarvis. We'll find him."

Thomas opened the door to go to his car with all his notes and photos. He was ready to get back to his desk and work on the case. Every case Thomas took was solved. He was a retired investigator from Boston, Massachusetts and wanted to go back to work again. Thomas settled in Seabrook and continued doing what he did best, solving cases. The phone call from the Brooks brought back the Boston days for Thomas.

Chapter 20

———— ⚬ ————

Marc arrived home from the weekend trip and checked his answering machine like he always did. There was a voice message, and he thought it would be from Brent about reaching Seabrook. But the message was unexpected. Jared was kidnapped! Everyone was shocked.

He replayed the machine to make sure he heard it right, but the news of Jared's kidnapping was true. Marc called Brent after hearing the terrible news, "What happened, Brent?"

"We don't know, Marc," He said hopelessly, "We arrived here in Seabrook at the airport. Jared left something in the helicopter, so he went to get it, but he never returned. We searched everywhere, and it is like he disappeared into thin air."

"Well, that's weird," said Marc.

"Who would do that to us? Who?" he said angrily.

Sundara was alarmed to hear everything. "Don't worry. We will find him," consoled Marc.

"Yeah, I hope. I would keep you updated. You stay by the phone, Marc."

"Sure, let me know if you need anything."

After this quick call, Marc Dazet just stood there thinking who would want to hurt them? I can't believe this! Suddenly, there was a knock on the door, and he went to answer it. No one was there he glanced to see, but there was no one. He shut the door and went down the hallway. There he saw two figures wearing black baseball hats, the same guys who followed him earlier.

"Hello Marc, can we talk for a few minutes?" one of them asked, *"You know who we are? We're from the Earth Surveillance unit, and we heard something has happened in New Hampshire."*

We're going send people down to finding out what's going on. Can you tell us what happened.?

"I don't know a thing, Sir."

Okay, take our card again. Call us if there is something that you can't handle. We would be near you," they said, handing Marc a card.

Sundara called Marc, but he didn't answer. She then came looking for him in the condo and saw two people leaving the hallway, and Marc stood there, shocked. He shut the door and walked in and said, "They know something is going on with Brent and they're going down there to find out. I must warn Brent."

Dr. Eugene called Brent, "Hello nephew, this your Uncle Eugene. How are you doing?"

"Uncle, they have Jared!" Brent blurted out.

"What are you talking about Brent?"

"Someone kidnapped my son, uncle!" There was a numbing silence on the other side.

"Uncle, are you still there?"

"It Has Started," he replied with a heavy heart.

"What has started?" Brent asked confusedly, *"Anyways, there was a lady who called here to trade Jared for the Relic."*

His uncle spoke sterner and look "Brent, give her this Relic. Do this now!" Dr Eugene's voice grew graver, "Do not get in any trouble with this lady. Just give her the Relic. We have to talk. You might want to sit down, Brent."

Is everything okay? Who is he? Do you know her!?" Brent sat down.

"I'll answer everything, just listen to me carefully. This lady is not from Earth."

"What?! Oh my god!" Brent was shocked.

"She is not from here, Brent. This is why I asked you to give her the Relic. You need to do this as soon as possible. Jared is in danger."

Soon the agents from the Earth Surveillance unit surrounded that area of Seabrook, New Hampshire to ask questions.

"Well, Margret has hired a Detective. He can help us out as well."

"Well, this is beyond the detective scoop, this not of human matters. I do not want him to get hurt. No one knows the capabilities of these beings. It's best to do what she says, okay?"

"Okay, Uncle."

"I feel everything will be back to normal after you hand her the relic. There is more, but I will stop here. Stay safe and call me if you need more help."

"Yes, I will be careful. I just want my son back."

Dr. Eugene hung up the phone and made another quick call. Brent walked out of his office, thinking about what made his uncle say that the lady was not from Earth. He was more vexed now, thinking about the type of harm she could bring to his son.

Brent worried about the news that his uncle gave, walked in, to the living room, he looked around at his at family watching their reactions. It felt as if the time has stopped. There was a call, and it was Yautja. He picked up the call, and it was the same voice that he heard the last time, "Meet me at the pier in an hour with the Relic — no one else but you. I can tell if there is anyone else with you. Your son will be on the pier. Once I have the Relic, I will release him to you." The call ended.

Brent pounded his fist on the cabinet. This had never happened to him.

"What happened, honey? Where's Jared?"

"She called to tell me to meet her at the Pier in an hour." His hands were shaking. He knew this was a crucial time because she was not from earth. She could have extra-terrestrial powers which can be dangerous. But Brent was determined to get his on back even if she was from Planet Krypton.

Yautja knew that by taking one of the twins, she could get what she wanted. She gave it a lot of thought about who to choose. Jared didn't know where he was as she had erased his mind. Without question, he put on the fishing clothes on Yautja's command. He wore a tan fishing vest and a hat with fishing trinkets on it. His disguise blended well according to the place. She said, "follow me," and he did. Jared had a blank look on his face.

It took about 15 minutes to get there. Her hotel was not too far from the pier. There were lots of avid fishermen and women on the dock that day. She had to dress them to blend in. She also brought fishing rods and a tackle box.

"Walk on the pier," she said to Jared. People were standing on the sides of the pier. She picked a crowded area and told Jared to stand there.

She moved to a different spot, closer to the beginning of the pier. She was carrying a Yeti cooler which mixed her well in the crowd. Yautja kept a close eye on her surroundings. Jared was standing in the middle half of the pier. People were catching stingrays, crabs and fish of all types from the ocean. It was a busy day at the dock.

Then she saw Brent parking his car and getting out. Nelson was in the car's trunk. Brent seemed hasty and anxious. He was walking briskly on the pier looking around, but he could not see his son. People thought he was crazy. Then he received a call, "Hello, I see you have made it. Now, take twenty steps forward from where you are."

He looked around to see if he could find who was making this phone call, but he saw no one. Yautja continued, "After you take twenty steps, make a right and then put the relic in the bag."

He counted his steps, made a right and returned after putting the Relic in the bag, as instructed. As soon as he made the drop, he heard a loud noise from the pier. Jared had snapped out of his hypnotic state and last memory in his conscious state which was him escaping from Yautja at the hangar. He stepped back and shouted at the top of his lung, "Keep your hands off of me!" and he swung his fist and arms at strangers on the fishing pier.

"Get it off of me now!" Jared struggled. The people next to him didn't know what had happened to the boy. Everyone heard him yell on the pier. Brent ran to him, shouting, "Jared! It's me, your Dad! Nelson ran out of the truck on to the dock quickly.

"He ran to untie him, "Jared, it's me. Wake up! Wake up!" Jared blindly looked around in his surroundings, looking at the ocean and people. After he regained consciousness, he saw Brent, and his senses returned."

"Jared, it's me, your father!"

Nelson surrounded Mr. Brooks and Jared for protection. Everyone there was clueless about what just happened. Yautja had the brown tan bag containing the Relic. Clenching the steering wheel and punching gas, she drove back to Florida to release the warriors trapped in the spaceship underwater.

Chapter 21

—❮ ❯—

Harold came home. Hannah greeted him and asked him about his day. To which he said, "Honey, I can't tell you what happened today."

Hanna confusedly looked at him and said, "It's okay honey, maybe you could tell me later." Hanna understood him. She and Harold before coming to this base had faced a lot of rollercoaster moments, had gone for shopping the commissary groceries on different bases, and also traveled to other places and met cultures other than theirs. Their family had to adapt to different areas and surroundings.

This military base was more advanced, but the same formula of adaption applied. Hanna was learning the new schedules of her family. Her job was to support her children and stand by Harold through thick and thin.

She was already making plans of bringing the past to the future she thought from their experience at Dairy Queen. Hanna felt that she would start small, to see how it would spread her philosophy.

There was one thing she liked to do, which was to save. Whether it was saving money or preserving history, she had three metal USB flash drives that she brought with her of all their travels. The flash drive contained all the pictures and videos of their life events and everything that they had been through and things that they had learned.

She called them "The Three Musketeers" encyclopedia for the family, for each of them. There were pictures, school homework of her children. She thought it was small in size and significance as well, but it was not.

To bring the blast from the past to the current times. She does all the saving to store memories and the happy moments of their history. She asked her children once, "Do you guys know who are 'The Temptations'?

Both Nolan and Zelda looked at her and said, "No, we don't."

Hanna told them, "It's a singing group from Motown Records." She thought her children should know great singers and events from the past from all backgrounds.

Hanna thought that the youth could learn from the past and teach future generations. For this purpose, the Three Musketeers had everything stored in it. There was a computer made of bamboo and a little metal in the room.

She inserted one of the Musketeers in it and looked up 'The Temptations.' And there it was, all the videos and the descriptions about Group. And then she clicked on a song called "Just My Imagination" (Running Away from Me)

Hanna looked around to see if anyone was around, but there was nobody in the room, so she turned up the volume and started dancing. She twirled her hands in a circle and slid across the floor during the song.

Harold walked into the room and joined her. It was a kind of like they were Temptations. Harold seemed to know more moves than Hanna. With the song, he was dancing in spins and lip syncing each word.

Zelda and Nolan were doing their homework reading over their class schedules. Nolan stated, "The Temptations are neat did you see how that dance in sync Zelda." I know it was neat Nolan. Focusing back to their goal. They wanted to get enrolled in school sports like baseball, swimming or the debate team. There were different sports on this undisclosed military base, some of which they had never even heard of. Nolan brought to Zelda to show her.

"I want to sign up for a game called Takako," he said. There wasn't a description for joining the teams, but Nolan had heard about in class, and he wanted to know more about this game. He checked the schedule to sign up for it. Zelda saw something for herself too, a game called Charrette seem to grab her attention as it was more of a strategy game.

Harold was getting things ready that he would need in the morning for work. It was dinner time, both Hanna and Harold liked to cook. The current base served quite different foods, and they were excited about trying these new flavors. Although they still loved their homemade lasagna dinners, Chicken Fajitas and BBQ the new items on the menu like Super Miso, Sea Vegetables and Syntel sounded delicious. Hanna decided to try Super Miso for dinner.

There was a buzz on an intercom system, and it was Colonel Mathews. Harold clicked on the button and answered in a jolly mood, "Hello, it's Harold here, about to eat Super Miso."

"Oh wow, this is the best dish that you'll ever eat. Your family would thank us every day for finding this Japanese dish. Makes sure you try it. I just called to see how we're doing with the training and all."

"Colonel, it has been a great learning experience for me, even in the first three days of training."

"It's just the beginning, keep an open mind. You will meet others here."

"I've met two people, one from the Navy and the other one from the Air Force. They seem great."

"That's good."

"Okay, Sir, thank you for calling."

"No problem. Stay focused," and the intercom clicked off.

Chapter 22

———————◖ ◗———————

Marc was sitting in his office, staring blankly at his laptop. He was unable to write any story because he was worried about the Brooks, hoping Jared was safe and also thinking about how could he help. He was entangled about how will he explain Brent about the blueprints? He wanted to tell them while they were in Yorktown, but he could not.

Marc had been protecting his family for years, and so he wanted to make sure that it would be safe to speak before he tells anyone. While lost in thoughts, he received a text from Brent saying, "I have my son back, Marc. Jared is back home with us. I didn't even see the person who did this. It was weird."

"I'm glad he's back. But what was so special about this Relic that they took your son? This whole incident is bizarre."

Brent texted back, "You're right."

After this brief text chat, Marc was daydreaming about his family, Sundara and Laura and his original family as well. His family was from Hershey, Pennsylvania which is home of the Hershey's Chocolates. He grew in an adventurous town with a population of fourteen thousand. He explored his city first and noticed that everything began with the word 'Hershey.' There was a Hershey High School, Hershey Museum, and Hershey Park- an amusement park and this town had the most delicious chocolates around.

His family took vacations, and on every other store, he would see his hometown represented on candy bars, and he felt if they can do it, I can be adventurous too and that's what he did. He went to college in California, and he married someone from a different planet than his own.

The person who invented this delicacy, was Milton Hershey, and he learned it in Lancaster, Pennsylvania then moved to Denver to learn more about Caramel and milk. He explored many places before coming back home to Pennsylvania, which is a small town, but it made it to the far-off places of Earth through its specialty.

Marc felt the same, and he followed the footsteps of Mr. Hershey. His favorite t-shirt was a dark orange, Reese's Peanut Butter Cup t-shirt. Marc always wanted to meet his wife side of the family even if they're from another galaxy. He hoped one day his dream of meeting Sundara's parents and visiting her planet could come true. Sundara occasionally reminded him of how beautiful her planet is by telling him stories of her world, the Triangulum Galaxy.

Marc, snaps back to the present, after hearing Amelia's voice. "Hello Marc, you seem a bit lost, are you okay?"

"Yes, I'm doing fine."

"Great. How's the regional bike trails story coming?"

"I was waiting for them to call me back. I have information from there. Give me three days, and I will have a story for you, Amelia."

Marc paused for a moment then said, "Amelia, as a journalist, have you ever written a story that became a part of your life?"

"Yes, many times, Marc. It was in the late '80s. Once I was reading a story about Rubik Cubes as I like riddles. I got so interested in the story that I had to meet the person who wrote the story. Being a reporter at that time, I enquired for his name and contact. Wanted to know more about the story and how to solve the Rubik Cube Mystery, I asked him if I could talk about his story in person. We met and talked.

With a cube in hand and we both tried to solve it and it was a great evening. Fifteen years later, he is my husband now. So, yes, I know some times you get involved in a story, and it unfolds in front of you. Marc, do you have some story that's growing on you?"

"It's grown, Amelia. The lottery winner story, we're really good friends now, and a lot is happening."

Amelia looked at Marc, "Well, take your time and be careful. If something's meant to be, it will happen on its own. Anyways, do make sure you get the Bike trail story in time okay. You have 72 hours for this riddle from King Lear, "Uncle, is the lunatic a gentleman or an ordinary guy?" I will leave you with this.

Marc pondered on another cool riddle from her boss. He wrote down the puzzle to solve it. It was time to head back home. He was driving on the interstate, noticing that all seven cities were growing. Then, in his rare view mirror, he saw that he was being followed again. This time, it seemed like they were just watching him. Marc didn't panic and continued to drive on an average speed. However, he called his Sundara for a warning, "Hey honey, how are you? Listen, I'm being followed again, but they're not doing anything. I just wanted to call in to let you know just in case."

"Please be careful, honey. They are watching us more now."

"Yes, you're right. Oh, I had to tell you Jared has returned to Brent."

"I'm glad that he's safe. Who would kidnap someone's son? Marc, a lot is going on. Others are here on a mission about water and hydrogen. I saw these words on the prints on the blueprint today. It's bigger than a chance for going back home, honey. There must be more to this mission. I think it time to approach Mr. Brooks and discuss the details with him as soon as possible."

He traveled until the road turned to the beachfront. And the followers did the same. He stayed on the phone with Sundara the whole time. Listening to every word she said. Honey, he does not know about us as a family, this could scare him."

Sundara devised, "What if we think of a plan, so we don't frighten him much?"

"Sundara, that's going to be difficult because of what's on the blueprints. Marc flashed back to the interview with Brent about what he saw on the TV channel underwater and their family trip to New Jersey.

"We may have to alarm him, Marc, and take a risk, but it's important. We must move forward."

Marc agreed.

"The Weather!" Sundara's voice cheered up, "We can connect it to the weather."

Marc thought about her answer. She was right.

"We can show them how the weather can change through our eyes."

"Yes, but we would have to do this in person. It's better to wait on Jared to make sure that he's okay."

Marc arrived home, Sundara hugged him and clicked off her phone when he walked into the door. She was relieved that he had come back safely. They continued their conversation.

"Yes. Weather… We have to figure out some explanation about the parts. Transporting them to Starlings Island."

Her Muscle Car seemed like a Nascar flying on the Interstate to Florida. Yautja had what she needed to open the underwater mystery. She thought about the warriors on the ship, wondering how long have they been imprisoned. The Relic would show her the answers.

Now that Jared was kidnapped, she came in from the ceiling the of the Helicopter Hanger to remove the clues that might lead to her. Yautja knew there's one thing Human like to do and that is to investigate. To her, humans were curious creatures who wanted to know the Who, What, When, How and What of every matter.

She found a room at the airport to keep Jared and herself during the day of the kidnapping. Yautja had planned this out months in advance with all the details. She removed Jared's thoughts and memory for this short period and replaced them with other stuff. She waited for the Brook family to return home from their trip.

She was making sure not to leave clues in one place. She left traces which directed towards two different directions in case the Brooks hired a private detective. She knew how the people on earth would react. Yautja carefully planned and thought about everything. The only thing she forgot to think about was the Relic and the power of the Relic.

This Relic sent out signals to an underwater spaceship and Brent's satellite TV. It had its own working and directions. And it seemed to point in the direction that it wanted to whoever had the Relic.

Now Yautja needed it to unlock the last component of an unknown spaceship which was deep underwater. It was where she was sent for a mission. She defined the word "Compass" in an instrument for determining directions as a standard compass does by keeping a magnetized needle that always shows magnetic north. It determined her directions for Florida and next for the ocean waters.

Chapter 23

Detective Reilly was sitting at his desk reading notes from the evidence bag from the Portsmouth Airport and the data team at the lab in the detective's office. He saw tire marks for Ford Falcon Cobra 351 V8 at the scene. Reilly always wanted a Ford Mustang Shelby 1965 GT 350 with silver exterior and two black strips going down the top of the car, and he got one the year he retired. Yes, he admired the car and make of the suspect's car.

Reilly went through his office notes looking for clues, and where to go next, but there were no DNA or hair fiber except the children. How is that possible? He thought. In most cases, if the victim's DNA is there, then the suspects are not too far from the crime scene, but the weird thing was that there weren't any footprints entering or leaving the crime scene. He called the Forensic Investigation Centre for more information. They said that they were still working on the case and will send more details later. "It looks like an unknown matter detective," the lady at the lab said, "We're not sure. We may have to call in the internal affairs department for this. Some of this is very new to us."

Walking up and down his office, he knew Jared was back home safe. But he wanted to know who did this. Just in case it happened again to someone else. He had a board with his clues displayed on it. There was a hole in the fence, yet no DNA. He then traced the car tires and thought maybe the kidnapper had stayed at some hotel in Seabrook. I can call them and inquire.

While checking in a hotel, one has to register the car. Reilly made a list of hotels in that area to call. He took out his cell and dialed 603-474-5757 the person answered the phone, "Hello Hampshire Inn, can I help you?"

"Yes, I'm Detective Thomas Reilly." As soon as he said his name, the clerk knew who he was. "Yes, how can I help you, Detective?"

"Thanks, I'm looking for a car owner that could have stayed there a couple of days ago?"

"Sir, what make and model can I check our records for?"

"It's Ford Falcon Cobra 351 V8."

"Okay sir, let me check." He went through the records and said, "No, sir, there wasn't any car of that model registered with us."

"Okay, thank you for your help and have a good day."

He hung up the phone, then thought if someone comes to Seabrook, they at least stay one night in hotels facing the ocean. Let me guess which one, he checked the list and came up with Ashworth by the Sea on Ocean Boulevard. He called the number, and a man answered, "Welcome to Ashworth by the Sea. Can I help you make a reservation?"

The Detective spoke, "Hi, I'm Detective Thomas Reilly."

It was a small town, so the front desk clerk knew who he was.

"I am looking for a car owner that might have checked in your hotel in the past couple days. Could you check on this certain make and model?"

"Sure sir, what is the model?"

"It's Ford Cobra 351 V8."

The front desk clerk looked through the records to see and came back to the phone, "Yes, sir, we had a similar car owner stay here a couple of days ago."

"What! Really?" The Detective stood from his chair, "Look, pull those papers out, I will be down there in ten minutes. He grabbed his jacket and left immediately. The clerk was holding the phone

115

shocked about what just happened. Ten minutes went by and pulling in like clockwork, and there was Detective Reilly. It seemed as if he jumped out of his car while it wasn't fully parked. The clerk let him in and ask him to come in, and he opened a door that went behind the front desk reservation desk.

Then, he pulled the records and Reilly, carefully observed these papers and there it was, the Ford Falcon Cobra 351 V8, registered under Melissa Scott Lago. The Detective wrote it down and asked for a copy of the paperwork. He looked at the name and asked, "Isn't Scotty Lago a famous Olympic snowboarder from Seabrook?"

"Yes, this is why I didn't pay much attention, I thought it was some relative of their family who had checked in."

"Did you get a photo ID of the person?

"Yes." He looked for it and handed it to the detective, "Here, she looks a bit older, though."

"Okay, I will take a copy of this photo too. Can I take a look at the room this person was staying in?"

"That room is currently booked, sir." The Detective thought, how can I get the family out of the room he thought about it and said, "I have an idea." Detective Reilly found the fire alarm button next to the door and pulled the alarm. He knew this would do it.

His plan worked, everyone in the room walked out and went to the beachside waiting for a fire department to show up to turn off the alarms. The Detective went in to inspect the place.

He searched the room in places many people would not look, as he was searching clues for the case. He looked in the right corner facing the windows, but could not see anything. The family had their items all over the room. He knew he didn't have much time, so he quickly checked the draws. While checking the draws, under one of them, he saw a glowing object. It looked otherworldly. He collected the item, thinking it might be a clue.

He had seen nothing like that before. The object looked like a nail or a screw of some sort. Soon, a fireman came into the room, "Sir, you are supposed to be outside when the alarm goes off, can you please leave so we can check the room?"

The clerk told the fireman that he was a detective, looking for something in this room. The fireman suspected Reilly of pulling the alarms? The fire alarms turned off. While Reilly was leaving, he could hear the voices of the guests returning to their room. He thanked the clerk and gave him fifty dollars for all his help. The Shelby car door opened as Reilly stored the only evidence, he had collected from this case back into his car. He started to drive back, wondering who this kidnapper is? Where are they from?

Jared was quiet. He didn't say much. The family surrounded him, and they were thankful that he was back home safe. Then he broke the silence and asked, "Who did this to me?"

The family started looking at each other, thinking the same thing. It was weird that Jared didn't know who did it. Everyone was expecting him to tell them about the kidnapper. Brent whispered to his wife, "He needs a little more rest. Maybe he is still in shock."

Jared must have overheard them, he said, "I can hear you, Mom and Dad. I'm not insane. I do not know who do this. All I remember is going back to the Helicopter hanger, and the rest is all blurry."

"Don't worry son. We have hired a detective to investigate the case. We also want to find out who did this to our family," Brent assured him.

"Yes, let's find out because if they do this again to us, I do not know what I would do to him, Jarvis said speaking louder than his usual tone. This incident changed him a lot. He was no more afraid to talk now.

Margret, on the other hand, wanted to call off the investigation as Jared was back now, but everyone else in the family wanted to find this person.

Brent missed his relic that was missing from his safe. He had been watching the relic for a while now since the trip to New Jersey. Brent thought he should call the Lenape Indians Chief and tell him what happened. He might direct them on what to do next. Brent told his family, and Margret agreed with him. She felt this gift that was given to their family was an honor. "Okay," Brent said, "I will call tomorrow. Right now, our son is my priority."

Jarvis was observing carefully. He was more focused and looked for details in everything, unlike Jared, who lived in the moment. If one asked about any past incident, Jarvis would explain it accurately. The brothers were born on the same day, yet they were so different.

Chapter 24

———✦———

Nolan and Zelda were now getting used to their new school. They were not only getting accustomed, but they also wanted to take part in school events. The sports at North Apex were different from regular schools. Both activities they chose were new to them.

Nolan walked outside after school to the ground where children were practicing games. He noticed girls and boys were looking the same, but the only difference was that everyone was wearing different shoes.

In class and outdoor sports activities, they always had different outfits here. They were far more advanced from the rest of the bases. When Nolan walked by this practice field, he noticed a sign which read 'Takako Practice Field.' He walked over to the ground and looked at a monitor that read off-grid training on the at-home simulator. And in person practice here at 3:30 pm on this field. There weren't many people out here, although it was almost 3:30, but he noticed some players, and their shoes stood out. He grew up with Nikes Air, Jordan and other brands like Rebooks, Adidas and, Vans. Everyone in school wore branded shoes. On this progressive base, the dressing and customs of inhabitants were also up-to-date.

After the classes, Renee and Zelda caught up with Nolan at the practice field. Nolan asked Renee if could she explain the game to him as he was interested in joining up for the team. Renee was happy to help, "It is a popular sport of our school, many of the top players are popular. The game is called Takako, and there are runners, two runners per team and they wear pads, helmets and cool suits. Each team has eight players, and they can be both girls and boys."

Nolan asked, *"Both girls and boys?"*

"Yes," she continued, "Every player wear's pads, and there's a flat carriage with a person inside and another who must pull the carriage across the field. Each team has three flat carriages and a puller."

Nolan was confused. She asked him to think of it as a High School team sport.

"So, there are two runners on each team, and they help bring and defend their three carriages and pullers across the field. Some people who play this sport are good at running and dodging the obstacles, so they play as pullers, and others who are good at directing traffic they sit in the carriage."

Nolan liked this game. He looked at the field and saw the players practicing.

"How do you win?" he asked. "Each carriage has to score three times, whoever makes nine home runs first wins."

"There's more to the game. Each home field has surprises that can happen while you're trying to score. Also, there is something that the runners get to help their team score and defend, I am not sure what it is, but I heard it was cool. It's an adventurous game to watch and play. Our first game is at 7.30 pm this Friday if you want, we can all go then you can see it in action."

Both Nolan and Zelda wanted to go to the game with Renee. Zelda asked Renee where she could find the Charrette Team. Renee like this activity, she thought if Zelda liked it too then maybe she can join with her.

"Charrette players meet on Thursday right after school. I will show you their practice area follow me," said Renee. They went to a dome area and walked inside. There no one there. At the end there stood a giant twenty feet screen with Giant digital markers on the side. Renee turned it on when she waved her hand in a cool noise came on and said, "Welcome to Charrette."

Nolan said, "There must be a lot of people who play this game."

"Yes, you can be on the High School Team if your good enough. Many people watch this game from home as well."

She told Zelda and Nolan to stand back and watch the screen. She put a device on her waist, turned it on she found the game and tapped play and clue, North Apex High School, and Renee drew a building on a giant screen which displayed an image in Hologram, then she clicked on sound, and the sounds of people walking around the building came to life.

Nolan and Zelda were in shock. Nolan said, "This is like a modern-day Pictionary."

Zelda guessed that it was the North Apex High School, the shape and the sounds were like there were two schools. She wanted to try it too, so she put on the waistband and looked at the giant screen. Like an ant looking at a human. The clue mentioned, "To Triangulum Galaxy."

Zelda looked at the clue and didn't know what to draw. She was clueless, but it seemed like whoever plays this game knew what the clue meant. She called out to Renee, "I don't know how to draw this clue on the screen. Could you help me, Renee?"

She came up, looked at the clue and knowing right away what it was. She drew in on the big giant screen. Zelda and Nolan just watched as the galaxy came into existence right before their eyes. When it appeared in the Hologram, they were stunned.

Renee knew that they were new from the look on their faces, as they saw the hologram and the sound vibrating their bodies. Renee generated this entire planet, "This is Triangulum Galaxy." "Really?" Nolan said, "That's a massive planet."

"Yes, both Triangulum and Andromeda are huge."

Both liked this game, but Nolan wanted to stay with making the Takako Team. Zelda wanted to join the Charrette high school team with Renee.

"Well, that's a lot for today, Renee. We better head back home now," said Nolan.

"Okay guys," Renee said, "I well see you tomorrow for school. I will tell you something that I know about this military base. As I was born here, I know the place very well. So, making good friends for me is fantastic. I'm glad I met you guys. I wasn't sure at. First, it's hard for me to trust others. But you guys are cool."

"We are glad to be friends with you too, Renee," they said.

Harold was home early, waiting for his children to get home. They were a little late than usual. But Hanna wasn't worried about them as the kids were allowed to be out before 5 o'clock. This was the magic number after which they went into action for searching Zelda and Nolan.

"Honey, they have a device like a cell phone, I can call to check up on them. One second, let me see how to use this device on the wall." Hanna looked at all the buttons, one of the buttons said, Nolan and Zelda. After selecting their name, it buzzed. Nolan had never received a call on his TC before, so he looked around and later realized that it was coming from his TC. The screen showed an incoming call from 'home'. Soon, Nolan picked up, and Hanna's voice came over, "Nolan is that you?"

"Yes, mom, it's me. We are heading home now. We got a bit late looking for sports teams. We both are okay."

"Okay, Nolan."

And he put his MC in his backpack, amazed at the technological advancement. After a little while, the bus dropped them off.

Chapter 25

―――――⋈―――――

S itting at his office in Hampton, Virginia, Dr. Eugene was looking over everything, also thinking about his nephew and Jared's kidnapping. He couldn't believe someone could do this to his family, but he was glad that he was safe now. Focusing on the plan, Dr. Eugene was thinking of some way to connect Brent and Marc. Just as he made sure the island was available when Marc was given the blueprints.

Time would connect the puzzle pieces together. Dr. Eugene was studying his notes, adding more details to the plan. He wrote the names of Joe and Tobias, knowing he would need both for carrying out his plan. He called Brent on the phone, "Brent, are you okay? Is Jared doing fine?"

"Yes, Uncle he's coming through now, but it seems as if someone has taken his memory away. He doesn't remember what happened during the kidnapping.

"Brent, you haven't spoken with your parents in a while, have you?"

Brent thought about the question, "Well, it's been of couple years since I've heard from his from them. However, when I won the Lottery, I sent funds to a mailing address." His Uncle knew they were time travelers like him. But he did not want to reveal this to nephew.

Then changing the topic, Dr. Eugene said, "No human can do that to a person, they must have been from different planets other than earth he thought."

"Yes, the detective is still on the case looking for more clues Uncle Eugene."

"How about you stay near the island for a while? You can get the construction started in the meanwhile and kids can also relax." Dr. Brooks had an agenda behind devising this getaway. "Yes, Marc's also down there with his family, they can help Jared recover." Brent thought about what his uncle was saying, and it made sense. "It's a good idea, this way I can stay out of the media and start on the island. I want to talk it over with everyone I'm sure they will agree."

"Okay, I will check in if you go to Starlings Island. Let me know, and I will call Marc. Take care. Talk to you soon." He took more notes after the call, writing visit Space Marine Infantry Base and then visit Tobias in 2048 and discuss the plans.

Brent thought about his uncle's plans and got the idea to contact the Free state project office, and it had been a while since they talked. His main concern was the wellbeing of his son. Starlings Island came second in his priority list. He spoke with his family, "I thought if we could all leave Seabrook for a couple of weeks and live near Starlings Island.

We can build there and grow the area for our family's needs. Laying low for a while would also keep them under protection. Nelson will plan our trips with security as a top priority. Moreover, we may not travel from the same airports and change locations to keep others who want to harm us off the track."

Everyone agreed.

Okay, guys, Nelson will be the only handling our travel arrangements. Jarvis and Jared would need to transfer to the new schools. Those schools may not be as big as the ones here, but it's just for little time. The school in Saxis are not too far from the Chesapeake inlet. We will share living areas here in Seabrook and Starlings Island." They all agreed to the new plans.

Yautja was passing through South Border of North Carolina. She liked the scenery of Interstate I 95. She thought to herself this road is very famous for humans, it is beautiful, indeed. As she drove listening to some music, she could feel the air on her face, which reminded her of the excellent music of Triangulum Galaxy.

She knew that she would have to pass by Savannah, Georgia then to Jacksonville Beach before going on to her destination in Florida between Pompano Beach and Fort Lauderdale, this was where she had to bring the Relic. She observed the ship from her car and saw that marine life growing around the spaceship as if it was their new home.

The distance was getting closer every mile that she drove. The Relic was now in her possession. She looked at it carefully to see if she had seen this in her past. She knew about two Relics of the past; one was the 'Phaistos Disc' discovered by a soldier of Italian origin. It was from the Minoan Bronze age, and the second one was the 'Rosetta Stone' found by a French earthling in 1799. The second relic had its origin from Egyptian history.

Now that Yautja was finishing her mission, she knew a lot about Earth and other places. She was now driving on the coast of Georgia at a reasonable speed. On the Kidnapping, she had to do what was required of her to find the Relic. It was a key, but she wasn't sure who's. She only knew it was meant to fit in the spaceship to unlock some warriors.

Rhonda Cayuga was listening to her elders as they were talking to others on the Wanaque Reservation. Something had happened. The Chief knew something was wrong. He said something to Rhonda to discuss details of the matter, but she couldn't quite understand his meaning. However, she could tell from the mood n gestures that things were not okay. The Lenin Lenape tribe was very spiritual in thoughts and practices.

The elders explain them to Rhonda, and she grew up with vast knowledge of the Wampum Belts. They were purple and white in color. There were messages inside the belts with five images.

The Wampum Belt was so crucial that at the time of the agreements between settlers and Native American Indians, these had a stronger influence than the agreement paper. Whatever was said on the Wampum belts, both sides understood and made a pledge on the belts. Most belt messages displayed hexagon shape telling of the history of that belt.

Rhonda grew up making herbal medicine from many types of trees and her natural surroundings to heal the wounds and treat diseases. Just as of today, most prescription comes from our outdoor surroundings, and so do our seasonings. The Lenape tribe were the first to work with such spices and drugs. They worked on these when there were no refrigerators. The Lenape learnt how to store their food for more extended periods.

The Chief asked Rhonda if she can call Margret. He felt that something was not right. She called her at once, "Hello Margret. It's Rhonda. How are you? Is everything okay there?"

Its surprised Margret that she had called during this time as if she knew something had happened beforehand.

"Yes," Margret answered hesitantly, she couldn't talk because she was upset, "I will put Brent on the phone."

Brent came on, "Yes, Rhonda, how are you?"

"I'm fine. How are you all? Is everything okay?"

"Actually, no, our son Jared was kidnapped last week."

"What?!"

"And the person wanted the Relic in exchange for Jared."

Rhonda was shocked. She told the Chief about the incident, and he came closer to the phone to hear more details on what happened.

"Yes, they called and said we want the Relic," Brent continued, "It's crazy. how did this unknown person know that we possess this Relic from New Jersey and the tribe of Lenape?"

The Chief spoke to her, and she translated the information to Brent. Chief said, "The Relic has a mind of its own. It will leave and come back to you, Brent. It goes in a direction that it's supposed to go, but it will come back to its spiritual owner. Please, go search for it, and at the right time and day, it will be in your hands. This is all I can say. Also, I am sorry for the kidnapping."

Rhonda was upset about the event, "There must have been a reason behind this, Brent. Do keep your eyes and ears open for such an event might repeat itself."

Brent agreed with her and told Rhoda to thank the Chief. Then he handed the phone to Margret, "Hi Rhonda, I'm back. Sorry, I was upset over what happened with my son."

"Don't worry. I will talk with the Chief and get more information about what's going on. They know a lot more than I know. I'm still learning, But I'll try my best, Okay Margret, Lapa Knawels, Williamson... Rhoda said in her Native Lenape language. She translated for Margret, feel well, to be in good health.

Chapter 26

—=( )=—

Yautja arrived in Florida around 3:00 pm. She was right on time as most of the tourists and residents are busy roaming around town instead of being on the beach. She looked at the device on her wrist to locate the ship's coordinates. Once found, a buzzing sound came from the gadget with a holographic map to guide her to the ship.

"I must get closer to the shore," so she drove down the main ocean drive till about 59th Street in Pompano Beach oceanfront. People had creative names for their homes like "Let Me Count the Waves" and "Barefoot Bumblebee." she keeps driving the 59th Street entrance to the ocean lovely two-story beach home.

Yautja needed a private entrance to the beach, so she chose to enter from one of the houses located on the oceanfront. After selecting a house, it seemed like no one was home, but she thoughts whether someone's home or not, I'm going in any way. So, she parked up on the road around the 63rd street. And she walked down back to 59th street.

She entered the beautiful two-story house. It seems like no one was home. She looked to see if someone was home, but there was no one. At 3:30 noon, she opened the gate leading to the ocean, looked sideways to see if someone was watching. Yautja then put on her special swimsuit, held the device in her mouth and ran towards the beach. Soon she was gliding on top of the water like a shark with fins and slowly went in the deep ocean. She had kept the Relic safely in her pouch.

She was going in deeper and deeper in the salty waters of the ocean. All wildlife swam away from her confusing her for a whirlpool. The closer she was getting to the location, the stronger the buzzing got.

It looked new even though she visited the spaceship before. The ship recognized Yautja as the main entrance of the ship swirled, and the water went into motion when she went to the middle. The lights from the door glared on her and the ocean water like a spotlight.

She went to the door, and the water current aided her. The current moved her up, and it must have taken ten minutes for this process to finish. This force of the water brought her to the main platform, and the entrance closed shut. She was now in a dry area, and surprisingly, she could breathe.

She stood up and checked her Satchel for the Relic. It was there. While in the spaceship, a small light turned on first, and then the bright lights lit up the whole spaceship. She found the way to go to the chambers where the time capsules were located. she grabbed a handle in the spaceship elevator and off it went. Poof! it was gone with speed, and a voice came on to tell her something.

Yautja was now in the room with time capsules and the people from different times. There were five capsules, and she looked at each of them and noticed one of them looked like her but older in age. Yautja could tell it was her.

How in the world did they do that? It's me! But an older me? Soon she found the section to place the Relic and put it in its proper place. Now, Yautja stood back to see what happens next. All of a sudden, it went completely dark. Yautja was alarmed, she kept watching the capsules. Then the light in capsules turned on. A noise came on in her native language, it seemed to give an introduction for each time capsule.

Yautja stood still in a corner and watched cautiously, the first capsule opened and one, two names came from the voice on the ship it said, "Welcome 'Set' and 'Comet'." A bird and an old man came out. He had a white beard and a circle in the middle of his forehead. He carried a knapsack. In just a few minutes, both became active.

Comet flapped its wings and looked around the ship. Set said something in Yautja's language, he tried to translate but it was an older version of her language. She thought, time must have changed how our people speak now.

The next capsule Opened, and the creature was introduced as 'Chi', and this one was different. Its colors were dark blue and purple, and he had an oriental type of hat on.

The next three capsules remained closed, but their names were mentioned in the introduction. The third capsule was containing 'Boji' and 'Eolu'. They were tiny in size and wore black frames with a red lens. They both were contained in a little in frame, Boji and his small pet, Eolu. They were bizarre.

The fourth capsule was introduced, didn't open the voice spoke "This is Yautja." She was amazed, "Whoa, that's my name. I was right." The last capsule was of 'Lunar-the Knight'. Two capsules were opened, but the rest remained closed. Yautja stood there in awe, watching them and thinking, what are they going to do? I have never seen this before. I have to be careful. Very careful.

Saxis Island has a population of 241 residents and very close to the island that Brent bought. It was where the Brooks had to stay while the construction on their island took place. Brent thought it would be a perfect place for their family as they could get to know the locals and the twins' schooling would continue. Moreover, he felt he could protect his family in a better way while staying Saxis temporarily.

There also was a fishing pier located there of about 200 feet long, which is a good spot for fishing trips and family bonding. The high school situated 16 miles away from Saxis Island called 'Tangier' had the strength of 66 students only.

It mirrored the same as their ocean town of Seabrook, New Hampshire. Nelson made the arrangements for the family to arrive via top-secret routes. The Brooks rode around Saxis island touring for their new home until their island was livable for their family.

Nelson made the plans to arrive top secret their travel routes and where they're staying. At last, they found a home. It kind of reminded them of Seabrook. Brent rented this guest house, which was not too far from the Starling island. It had three bedrooms with an extra room for Nelson.

The house had a nice feel. This was very new to them, living in a new place for some time and building a new home from scratch. However, they all felt safe here as they knew nobody and nobody knew them. Jared seemed at ease now and was talking more. He was trying to jog his memory to find out what happened to him at the airport, but it was still very blurry. Detective Riley called them every now and then to check up on them and tell them if he found any clue.

Brent wanted to call Marc and tell him that they were in town, but he was waiting until Thursday. The phone rang to Marc. He picked up, "Hello Brent, how are you?"

"Hey Marc, I am good. You're not going to believe what I am about to say."

"I guess it's good news?"

"Yes, we're in Virginia. I wanted to see if you could come to visit us tomorrow or the day after?"

It surprised him, "Wow, that's a great. Yes, I can visit tomorrow."

"Great. Make sure you bring your family too. I'll text you my address."

"Okay, I will. See you tomorrow then. Take care."

Marc explained to Saundra about going to Saxon. "They came down here all of a sudden, I think it was for the family's protection," said Saundra.

"It's smart to do that, honey."

Marc honey, maybe we should tell them about the blueprints now."

"Yes, this is the right time. We should show them the blueprints first."

Both Marc and Sundara planned to meet the Brooks tomorrow. Marc said, "We must tell their family, but it has to be in small steps, so they don't get alarmed."

I feel we might be contacted from home, Marc, Sundara mentioned, "I have a feeling a lot is going on." Both of them went over the plans together for what and how to tell the Brook family.

Chapter 27

———⦿———

Next day Sundara and Marc arrived at Saxon, Virginia with their daughter, where the Virginia wind was blowing. Brooks Family's Guesthouse was not too far from their place. Marc looked at Saundra with an assuring gaze that this is they reveal their secret and plan. Being a news reporter, it was his job to tell others about news and reveal secrets and stories.

But he had kept this story to him kept for a long time. And now it was time to tell it to another family. It was a relief to him and Sundara because now they would be able to share and discuss things with them.

Marc noticed right away this was not Brooks family home in Seabrook, New Hampshire the size of this house was smaller, it must be their temporary residence. He pulled into the driveway and parked his car. It didn't take long before Nelson and Brent went out to greet them in the driveway, "Hi you guys, you made it here quick."

"Yes, it's not too far from Virginia Beach. Your New England accent may soon change to a Virginian one," Marc said jokingly.

"Ahh… never, I'm still from New Hampshire even if I was on Mars." Brent replied. Everyone was outside greeting each other, and it felt like a family reunion. The wind was getting stronger, and Marc turned to Sundara. Then all of a sudden, the wind stopped, and everyone froze. Brent was the first one to say something, "What was that? The wind just stopped blowing abruptly."

Nelson felt it too, "Yes, what was that?" He could not be a bodyguard when it came to the weather. Everyone started walking towards the house, and the wind came back within a second and all of them noticed this. They walked in, and Margret and Twins were there. They greeted the guests and were happy to have people they knew for a change.

"Hi Jared, are you Ok?" Marc asked.

"Yes, I'm doing better."

"Sorry that something like that happened to you. There are some crazy people in the world, as well."

Jarvis agreed as he shook hands with Marc and Sundara. The twins were happy that Laura came too. Now they could talk about the current events happening in their age bracket.

"There must be a change of pace here in this small town."

"Yes, our island not too far away. There are about 241 residents here. Our town is small.

Then both Brent and Marc went to another room to talk.

"Brent, it's nice to see you here. Building your own island must be exciting."

"Yes, absolutely."

"Brent," Marc said hesitantly, *"I have to show you something, do you mind?"*

"Sure, what going on?" Brent asked.

Before reaching the Satchel that he brought, Marc first stared at Sundara. She gave him an affirming look, and he slowly pulled out the blueprints. Marc lowered his voice and said, "I wanted to share this with you. One day someone left this on my desk, so I it brought home."

Brent was looking at them with a puzzled face, "What are they?"

"They are blueprints."

"For what?" Brent asked.

"Well, they are blueprints for…" and then there was a pause.

131

Brent looked at him for an explanation.

"These are the blueprints for building a spaceship," Marc told Brent what he knew.

"Oh my gosh! How did you get those? Where are they from?" Then at that moment, he thought about his Uncle Eugene telling him something about to happen and to keep an eye out for things. So, Brent asked, "What you want to do with the blueprints, if I may ask?"

"Well, I was thinking… You now have an island of about 75-95 acres, so I was thinking, what if we build this here?"

Brent's eyes widened, and he looked around the room as if someone was hearing them talk.

"Yes, I thought we could build this spaceship from the blueprints."

"Whoa! No one has done that before." Then he asked Marc, "After we build this spaceship, what are we going to do with it? What if we get caught flying it in the air? I have never heard or seen anyone build a spaceship in my life, Marc."

There was a long pause. Marc didn't want to tell the other half of the plan.

Nelson knocked on the door to check on Brent, "Are you, okay sir?"

"Yes, we're okay."

"How are you doing Mr. Reporter?"

"I'm doing fine, Nelson," Marc replied, putting the blueprints back in the envelope.

Sundara was talking to Margret in their rented living room. She was asking her how it felt to be a lottery winner.

"I'm still the same as I was before we won the lottery. When Jared got kidnapped, I wished my husband didn't win the lottery if it's going to bring harm to my family."

Sundara understood what she said.

"But sometimes I like it too," Margret continued, "Here we are, getting ready to build on an island that we own. I would have never even thought of buying an island before winning the lottery. Just five years ago, I was teaching History in a High School, and my husband worked at Lowes Hardware store. However, we are trying to take it easy on the twins to keep them grounded to handle life.

Marc and Brent continued to talk after Nelson left the room. "Yes," Brent asked, "How will we get the material for this and how will we transport the material to the Starlings Island." Deep down, he liked the idea. It was different. He was amazed by the whole plan. Being a UFO enthusiast, he couldn't believe this idea fell so perfectly in his lap.

Marc said, "Maybe your Uncle could help us with the project, he knows a lot of people, you know." "Yes, he does. He knows more people than I have met in my whole life."

"There's more that I must tell you, Brent." Brent looked puzzled. "Can I make copies of these blueprints?" Brent asked.

"Not now, I just wanted to ask you about the idea first."

"I like the island, there's a lot of details, but we can work that out. I have the money to build this Marc, but the building material and its transportation are almost impossible."

Both walked out of the room to sit with everyone. Jarvis and Jared looked up.

"How are you guys doing?" asked Brent.

"We're good, but Dad, are you okay?" the twins asked.

"Yes honey, you look pale, Is everything okay? Margret asked Brent.

"Yes, yes, I'm okay. It must be the changing weather," he covered up.

The heat was on, and the house felt cozy. Then out of the blue, the temperature dropped. It was freezing cold, everyone looked around and was thinking what's going on.

"Did the heater break?" Jared asked.

Then a gust of cold wind swirled inside their home, and they knew this was

133

unreal. Jared looked around, "Oh my gosh, what's going on? We have the wind in this house just as we're sitting in an open ground."

Then Sundara said out loud, "I will stop this one." She stood in front of everyone, and the temperature went back to normal on her command. Everyone in the room except for Marc and Laura looked at Sundara like she was an alien, they were even scarred. Nelson was spellbound thinking how she did that.

Brent was worried, he asked her "Okay, who are you? Are you here to harm our family?"

"No, I need your help. I'm not from planet Earth."

Everyone took a step back, and Margret panicked as she had never witnessed something like this ever. Jarvis said, shaking, "Can you change the weather again?"

Sundara said "Yes, I can. Watch…" and then the wind blew in their home and it was cold again. Nobody cared for the weather this time. They were all numb after watching Sundara's power.

Then she switched the temperature back to normal and continued telling her story, "Marc and I are married. We have been married for some years now. However, we have never told anyone of this." Brent's hands were shaking when he asked where was she from.

"She said, I'm from a place called Andromeda Galaxy." Everyone listened to what she was saying. It was an instant moment like the Chief of the Lenape tribe talking to them in New Jersey. "Are you part of the ship I saw underwater on the satellite TV?" Brent asked Sundara

She said, "No, I'm not from there. I'm from a planet called Ooynt. And I feel in love with Marc, and we need your help."

"Look," Brent said, "We're not sure what to say now. It's a lot to take in for one day. How about you let talk as a family, and then we can talk more about it soon?" Brent voice was shaking while talking.

Marc agreed, and they showed themselves to the door. Sundara, Laura and

Marc walked out slowly to their Jeep and took off.

As soon as the door closed, everyone reacted to the strange discovery. Brent didn't tell the rest of the family about the blueprints, yet it was still on his mind. The twins were stunned, "No way! No way! Did you see that? She changed the weather in our living room from cold to hot and then back to cold." Nelson couldn't believe it too, but he was not that shaken as he was hired by Dr. Eugene to protect his nephew. He had seen such unbelievable things happen while working for him.

Chapter 28

———◄ ►———

arold's training never stopped. He trained at the barracks as well as at home. Last month he was with the Space Bravo Backward Unit B.W., but this morning he went to Commander Jacob Scott's Space Bravo Water Spartans Unit. Since Harold was a good swimmer, he felt that he would be okay going there. He reported to a dome. His unit was there outside of the Dome Barracks. This dome seemed huge. One could imagine by just looking at what their unit about a train for. Commander Scott was on time.

They were talking, and they heard a voice saying, "Ten-Hut Space Bravo Water Spartans!" and everyone went into formation. "Welcome to your first training class! What you are about to see here take in strides. It will take you a while to adjust to what's inside the Water Spartans training Program."

I want to tell all interns that this is 'Keeper of The Sea.' When you are leaving and entering this dome. Okay, Fallout. Let go and let go. Each one of us entered the Dome and said the new motto to enter this huge water area.

Harold was tenth in the line, and he noticed that this dome was huge, 86 feet high and 278 feet in size. As the soldiers were advancing, everybody was gasping at the size of it. Even Sub Lieutenant Max Gonzalez was surprised. For being in the Navy, swimming is a must so before joining. He was a lifeguard in California for many years. He knew the water well. Everyone was amazed as there was no water or any pools, the floor was flat. There were doors everywhere in this dome.

The Commander said, "Waters Spartan! Here you will learn how to swim better and in non-earth environments. Also, how to define yourself in these environments. I want to introduce one of our pools…" All of a sudden, the floor moved, and water started to fill in the pool. The floor shaped to an Olympic size swimming area before their eyes. On the left, there were the swimming gears for everyone with nametags.

The commander kept talking, "Proceed to the locker unit. Find and wear whatever's is in your locker. You have ten minutes. Go!" Everyone ran to the locker area. Harold saw his name '2nd LT Harold Johnson Water Spartans' on a locker.

Harold locker opened themselves in front of him and he looked in and saw varies swimming gear, there was a water helmet and swimming trunks he looked at the swimming pants and noticed a pulled down button that said the word Gravity.

In ten minutes, everyone was ready to go. The Commander told the soldiers to Jump in the water, and they did. "Now I want you all to swim a lap on your own. No order or timing is required. A buzzing sound would tell when you're done. I just want you to get used to this water."

Harold started from the end of the pool and swam. It felt refreshing, swimming the splashes in-between the paddling of feet. He still had the speed he use to have when he swam for the swim team. Some were better than Harold and some not so good. After completing the first task, the commander asked everyone to assemble in the middle of the pool.

All of a sudden, a roof came over, and side walls supported it making a room in the pool. Then the room moved up in the air the, and the soldiers exchanged strange looks, as the pool and soldiers slowly ascended in air.

Then a voice out of nowhere spoke, "Artificial gravity swimming seniors facilitate." The bottom of the pool slowly detached from underneath their feet. The supporting pool walls dispeared, the soldiers felt weird that the bottom of the pool disappeared and the pool water turned into a massive ball with no walls, floating in air. Like a rocket in space, only this was happening in a swimming pool.

Harold kept looking down. He couldn't believe that he was floating in a bottomless pool. All of them had worn the air-breathing helmets. While in the water, the commander jumped in from somewhere, and he told them not to panic. He asked them to push the air-breathing button so they could breathe. The commander said, "You are experiencing the artificial gravity swimming. This is how it will be on other planets where you may have to go. Their water is unlike ours."

Suddenly the pool water started rotating, and the commander told them to swim with the rotating flow of the water.

Then he told the soldiers to swim to the middle of the circle where there was air just as fine as outside. This part was known as a hubcap. The hubcap in this pool is the surface of the pool's middle.

Then the voice said, "Gravity Sensors Restoring," and the pool's walls and bottom reappeared. The soldiers cheered as if they had won a football game. The Commander then said, "Okay, Water Spartans, that's all for our training today. We will see each other on Tuesday. We have a whole year for your training of becoming a true Water Spartan.

When you all have changed, make sure to say the 'Keepers of The Sea' on your way out. Everyone couldn't believe what just happened. He checked to see if everything was intact. Harold now wanted to head back home and spend time with his family. He liked the advancement of the base and his training, but the family was still his first priority.

"Hi Honey, are you doing April?" Harold called Hanna's nickname.

Hanna answered back, "I'm okay. How is your training going?"

"It's going great. I've seen some unbelievable things while training. I think we need to have a family night to catch up with everything. Let's make it tonight?"

"Okay, I'll send out the flyers," Hanna said in a joking way.

The memo went out quickly to have a family night in the Johnson's living room. All four of them sat in their new living room. Harold opened the talk. "Okay family, how has it been going for you all? We have a Pow Wow tonight! Zelda, you're up first. Stand up and tell us what's been going on in your life lately."

Zelda stood up and spoke, "We made a friend at school. Her name is Renee Wiser. She was adopted, and she grew here." Hanna listened and thought that adoption and growing up on the same base was a rare case.

Zelda continued, "She has treated us both nicely. Now, Renee is showing us how things work at the school like a tour guide."

"How about your classes, Zelda?" Harold asked.

"There okay Mom. The classrooms are very advanced. We're learning from teachers as well as from students belonging to different places. We have a Tiny-computer (T. C.) that we have with us at all times as an assistant. We can consult it whenever we need help.

"That's cool. Can we see your assistant?"

"Sure," she switched on the TC , and a voice came on, "Hi! I'm Mims, Zelda's assistant."

Harold and Hanna were surprised at the enology. "I have one too!" Nolan said, turning it on. "Hello! I'm Hinge. I'm Nolan's assistant."

"These are incredibly helpful gadgets. You kids would learn a lot this way with technology," remarked Harold and Hanna.

"Nolan, what's happening with you?" asked Hanna.

"Well, I've been taking school classes, and after school, I wanted to take part in a sports team that I like. It's called 'Takako.' Their first home game is going to be this Friday night. I wanted to ask you if I could go?"

"Sure son, you may take your sister as well. Just make sure that you're studying. Stay focused and watch your peers. Your motto is "To Learn and be Stern."

Both agreed and listened carefully to their father. Hanna added, "We're going to cook together next week on family night, okay?"

Nolan and Zelda happily agreed. Hanna and Harold were glad that the current base had people from different nationalities as its good for the children to learn from all cultures and to intermingle.

"I wonder who would want to go from this base?" Hanna asked, "Is there any way we could call a family member to the base?"

"Yes, but it's an honor that they have chosen us to help our earth. So, let's help, learn and teach others who we are too."

"Okay honey, let's do it!"

Chapter 29

———————— ❊ ————————

The Brooks family sat in disbelief. Margret said, "She changed the weather five times, and made the wind blow from one side to the other." Jarvis and Jared sat there without their gadgets and headphones, which was a rare sight. Everyone including Nelson sat there in shock of what just happened.

"Why didn't we see the last time we meet them? Margret asked.

"You can't tell where she's from. She blends in really well. It's undetectable, honey."

Margret agreed.

"There's more. Marc showed me some blueprints to build a spaceship. He asked me to build it on our new island. I didn't give him any answer yet. Maybe that's why they came here and revealed their identity."

Nelson asked, "What if you help in this plan, and someone tries to harm the family again?"

Brent thought about it and said, "Yes, I know that we still do not know who kidnapped Jared, but uncle Eugene told me that something different would happen. What if it's the fate of our family to help them? After all, we have the resources."

Margret being protective, asked, "What is this spaceship supposed to do after we help build it? Should we call some higher authorities to tell what's happened today?"

"No Honey, they are our friends, and we don't want to be in the spotlight. Especially after the kidnapping incident, we can't afford it."

"Yes, you're right, honey. So, we'll need to start with making the island functional. We need water and utilities first." Brent suggested, *"I thought about a solution when I saw something in Saxis, Virginia. It is called The Solar City, they provide solar power to residents, and this can help us save a lot on the island. Their main electric source is A & N Electric."*

Maggie wrote everything on a notepad.

"As far as the water utilities are concerned, the country provides this service to the residents to have clean and fresh water. These are the first items that we need," Brent told his family.

Jared was still thinking about Sundara, *"Dad, that the lady made wind in this house. I can't believe how she did that."*

Jarvis paused, but then he stood up and said, *"Let's do it, Dad. Let's help them build this spaceship."*

Everyone in the living room was surprised at Jarvis. One of the reasons was that he was a quiet and reserved person who usually didn't speak up in such discussions and the other being that he stood up for the unthinkable.

Brent and Margret were shocked, so they asked, "Tell us one good reason to help them, Jarvis." "Well Dad, you have won the lottery which gave our family a second chance. We should give another chance to their family as well. We should help them but also keep ourselves safe.

Jared joined in, "Yes, we should help them."

Brent and Margret thought about what this and then agreed to go with the plan. Brent got up and called his Uncle Eugene.

Hey uncle, it's me, Brent. I want to tell you something strange that happened today. I will try to explain you, do you remember once you said that things are going happen soon and that I would be meeting new people so I have to keep my eyes open for what might happen?

"Yes, son."

"Well today, my reporter friend came to see me with his family. The reporter from the Virginia pilot newspaper who came to interview me about the lottery winnings."

"Yes, I can recall."

"Uncle, his family, wife and daughter both are not from earth."

"What!" Dr. Eugene pretended to be surprised.

"Yes, and that's not all. They asked us to build something on the island. After giving much thought to it we decided to agree on their plan."

Dr. Eugene knew what the "Something "was. As Brent keep talking. "Go on, nephew," he said.

"We're going to need your help. Uncle. Can you help us with this project?"

"Yes, I will help you with this project."

"Great, this was why I called you. I can't do this without your help. We're going to work on bringing power and fresh water to the island at first."

"Okay nephew, I will look into it and call you soon," said Dr. Eugene and the phone hung up.

Dr. Eugene wasted no time and called Rollins and Rollins, an unknown number that only he knew. A lady answered the phone, Rollins and Rollins-Expect the unexpected. How may I help you?

"Yes, this is Dr. Eugene Brooks."

"Hi there, Dr. How are you?"

"I'm good. I wanted to tell you that it's the time to call Joe Lewis and start the plans for the Island. A good driver would help transport the items to the island. We would also need some other people to help unload them."

"Ok," she said, "I will contact Mr. Lewis right away. And Dr. Eugene, don't be a stranger, call us more often."

"Sure, I will."

Then he hit a button opening the map of Eastern shoreline with details of the interstates, pick-up and delivery routes with time zone listings. He had a plan to the Starlings Island and routes by cargo boat with roads exits near and around the surrounding areas. He then thought about the builder of the spaceship, names were crossed off on his list, except one name, 'Tobias.' He was the only one who could do the job, and that was him. Paper and digital devices were scattered all over his desk. He knew there was a lot more work to, and he needed certain critical thinkers to make things happen.

Marc and Saundra were driving back home in their Jeep. There was no music or any sounds. Even Laura was sitting speechless on the backseat.

Then Marc spoke, breaking the silence, "What have we done Saundra? We told someone about our family. We have kept this secret from people for years, and now someone knows... She assured him, "We told the Brooks family, honey. They are not bad people. We have to wait and see the outcome."

However, Saundra did feel guilty. She couldn't even make eye contact with Marc and kept looking at the road on their way back home. "Maybe they will forget about what happened," she said as if to console herself secretly.

"Never, Saundra. We showed them your power of controlling the weather."

Laura jumped in their conversation, striking a ray of hope, "Maybe they agree to help us. If you guys ever think about that, there's a fifty-fifty chance." Laura kept her optimistic side. Marc kept driving, his mind drifting now and then from the incident to the riddle that his boss told him, "Uncle, is the lunatic a gentleman or an ordinary guy?"

At the gas station while filling up his Jeep, Marc told the cashier the riddle, who appeared rather nerdy and luckily, she knew the answer.

"Well sir, I have heard this riddle before, from King Lear. The answer is:

No, he an ordinary guy who got a gentleman for a son, since someone would have to be crazy to let his son become a gentleman before he's Achieved that distinction himself.

Marc thought about the answer and went back to the Jeep and said to his wife, "Honey, we're going be all right. Don't worry."

Saundra and Laura felt better after Marc's statement. They arrived home, now waiting impatiently for getting a call from the Brooks.

Chapter 30

———————————✕ ⟩————————————

Both teams were hard at work trying to solve the puzzle when the Crusaders finally figured it. The glass case opened to reveal sparkling shoes, with both teams grabbing their share and sprinting toward their lines. Two members from each team put on the shoes, with each runner donning a pair.

The glass cases, abandoned in the middle of the field, went back inside the ground. Both moved quickly towards the players, waiting for them to change into the new shoes. One of our runners ran in front of the puller player, clicking on a button located on these futuristic shoes, and they went 'up in the air'. It didn't lift too far up and could be maneuvered both sideways and forward.

The other runners followed suit and began testing their shoes. A countdown was ticking down from 50 in the background, while the band played throughout the testing period. The crowd cheered once they put the shoes on.

No one except the runners had these special shoes. However, everyone was curious to see what would happen after the countdown ended. It was down to 20, and then down to 15. The crowd was cheering with increased fervor, "Go Crusaders Go!"

The teams were ready, waiting for the countdown to end. The crowd counted in unison as it hit ten, nine, eight. When the countdown ended, a female runner began gliding in the air, followed by a player from the opponent team. Below, the pullers were ready to pull the flat carriages with long handles. One went first while two stayed back. The carriages were lifted in the air when the puller went left, and right due to aerodynamics.

Three periods make up a full game of Takako. Each team has the option to utilize its particular number of players each period. For the very first, the Crusaders brought out one Puller, one of the Fiat Carriages, and a Runner. Their opponents, the Moon Rise Rockets, decided to match them with two Pullers, two Fiat Carriages, and one Runner.

The crowd's excitement had reached a fever pitch. Nolan put his hands up in the air, gesturing towards Renee seated next to him. He showed her the "Why" symbol. He was wondering exactly why did the Crusaders bring out one team, while the Moon Rise Rockets placed two on the field of play. He soon learned why, with Renee explaining the facts to Zelda and Nolan in the stands.

> *"The Runner for each team can turn off their opponent's Fiat Carriage to take them out of the game. Once the Carriages are turned off, that leaves one less team for the whole period."*

> *"Really" Nolan responded back*

> *"Yes, they can," Renee answered matter-of-factly.*

The Moon Rise Rockets marched their two teams right down the middle of the field, with their Runner still hovering above. The Pullers gripped the Fiat Carriage tight as their teammate inside sent hand signals to the Pullers and the Runner in the air. He signaled a play they were about to execute on the field, at top speed.

The Apex Crusaders decided to do the opposite of the Rockets. Their strategy involved making use of the sidelines down the left-hand side of the field. They felt running down side line would be more fruitful due to lesser obstacles. Each Takako playing field had its built-in obstacles to make it harder for teams to score.

One thing the Crusaders failed to factor in was the fact that the Runner for the Moon Rise Rockets was a "star". Quick, agile, and aggressive, she was called "Ms. Zoom Zoom". Everyone on her team knew her quite well, and the fans had made chants in her owner. For every hand movement, filled with her greatness, the sounds came Zooooooom Zooooooom, with hands flying in the air like rockets. Nolan took an interest in her and focused on her playing talents.

While they were in the air, Ms. Zoom Zoom attempted to block the female player of the Crusaders towards the left. She froze in midair and somersaulted over the incoming player. The Rocket side of the crowd chanted her name, while the band played a small song to further liven up the crowd. Nolan wore glasses that allowed him to see the Runner's point of view, just like they allowed him to see the Puller's. The atmosphere was electric, with the crowd cheering their hearts out.

The Rockets then quickly released their second team into the air to confuse the Crusader's Runner. The crowd waited with tense breath to see the result of so many teams playing at once. For Nolan, each second he watched increased his desire to be on the team himself. He continued to watch the Crusaders' Runner, who came down to the ground to help the Puller cross the Carriage from the midfield. Her special shoes gripped the field and also allowed her to kick away opponents while in the air.

The Crusaders looked all set to score when one of the Rocket's Runners, Ms. Zoom Zoom, reached down and pressed the button which rendered the carriage useless, right before they were about to score. The Crusaders fans booed them for using two runners against their one.

The Crusaders' Carriage and Puller jumped off the field, leaving behind two Carriages. Soon enough, the digital scoreboard displayed: Crusader 0, Moon Rockets 1. The Rocket's band played their fight song, and their crowd went ballistic. Nolan admired there star Ms. Zoom Zoom.

Both teams had a five-minute break before they went back on the field. Zelda and Nolan were so mesmerized in watching Takako that Renee had to point something out to them.

"Here come the cheerleaders. Watch this, guys. It's very interesting," she told them.

Both Zelda and Nolan fixed their eyes toward the bottom of the stadium. It was the first time they had seen such a thing. All 12 cheerleaders had made their way to a platform adorned in the Maroon and Green forest outfits; the Crusaders colors.

Everything seemed normal to them until it all took another direction and the large platform floated up into the air with all 12 cheerleaders on it. They performed a Pyramid cheer on the floating platform, each standing on another's shoulders to form the diamond shape. They yelled out each letter in C.R.U.S.A.D.E.R.S, leading to huge cheers from the crowd. Zelda and Nolan were their loudest admirers among the crowd.

Nolan and Zelda Johnson realized they were not in Kansas anymore. Renee turned to them and explained that there's more to watch after this. The platform continued floating in the air and slowly made its way towards the fans. Then, the unexpected happened. Zelda yelled for Nolan to look as the platform hovered down close to the ground, not yet touching it.

Every cheerleader jumped down and took their place. Then, the entire platform detached into twelve smaller hover platforms. It was unreal and made Zelda and Nolan stand up to watch. They stared in disbelief and excitement. Renee yelled out, asking if they liked the visuals. Nolan excitedly yelled back his appreciation.

Each cheerleader had a single platform to themselves, just large enough to accommodate them. Right after that, chants of Let's Go Crusaders rang out in the entire stadium.

The game restarted as soon as the break ended. This time, each team had two Pullers, two Fiat Carriages, and two Runners, with the score 0 to 1.

It was the second period, with the crowd cheering their respective times. This time, the crowd raised the volume when the Crusaders' Puller made the first move. Soon both Runners were zooming through the air. The action confused Nolan, and he couldn't decide which camera he should choose. Runners lined up both sides of the field. The Crusaders' Puller felt like a flash of lightning as he ran through the field. The Rockets sent out a Runner in response, while the other one stayed back. As soon as the Crusaders Puller reached the middle, he turned the Carriage sideways to make sure the opposing Runner didn't hit the kill switch.

In fact, the Crusaders were waiting for the Rockets' Runner to make it to the middle. Just as he did, they struck the Rockets Carriage from both sides in midair. The Rockets' player fell to the ground and the Crusaders scored, turning off the Rockets Carriage. The score now showed Crusader 1, Moon Rockets 1 a tie, as the Crusaders supported erupted into volcanic cheers. It was all just exhilarating.

Another five-minute break ensued, but the bands continued playing. Nolan and Zelda were screaming so loud during the second period that their throats now ached. It was so much more fun to see Takako in action. Each team was now left with one Fiat Carriage, one Puller, and a Runner. During the break, one of the Runners pressed a button and her shoes cleaned themselves. This amazed Nolan as he saw it through his glasses. He wondered where he could get a pair of such shoes. He zoomed in to see the brand and make of the shoe, catching the popular 'GFG' etched on the side.

Both teams were now focused on scoring this quarter and securing their win. If they both scored, it would go into overtime, which neither team wanted.

The game was about to start again, with the Rockets sending there Runners into the air. The Crusaders responded by sending one into the air while the other one stuck to the ground, running with the Puller and the Fiat Carriage. The Crusaders' crowd drowned out the opposing one with sheer volume. As soon as the game resumed, the field began rotating in a circle. Metal cones could be seen all across the field. This period was a challenge for both teams as the field could rotate at any team. The new obstacles only increased the crowd's fervor and they erupted into volcanic cheers.

The Crusader Runner on the ground was male, while the one in the air was female. The former dodged each cone with ease and helped guide the Puller across the field. The Rockets responded similarly, but with both Runners in the air. The Crusaders' fans thought they were at an advantage since the ground Runner helped direct the Carriage across the cone-laden field. It was an extra pair of eyes after all. The Rockets took note of the Crusaders Carriage's progress and sent both of their Runners after it. However, whenever the Crusaders' Runner went right, the Puller took the Carriage left. It confused the Rockets to no end.

They tried to form a move, with the person inside the Carriage skating closer to the front and leaning forward to direct his fellow teammates. Everyone leaned forward to increase their speed. However, the Puller of the Rockets was now fatigued. This changed the momentum of the game. All Crusaders players were now on the ground fighting to score. Their Runners zipped through the field, dodging cones and opponent Pullers, as they helped their Carriage and Puller cross the line to score. The Crusaders had finally won. The crowd rushed to their feet and jumped into the air, yelling their appreciation. The applause could be heard for miles as the Crusaders took the game 2 to 1.

Zelda and Nolan were the happiest of the bunch. They were jumping and cheering their team right until the very end, yelling "Go, Crusaders!" at the top of their lungs.

Chapter 31

"Hello, Detective Thomas Reilly." Two dark figures from the Earth Surveillance Unit hovered over his desk, "We heard that you have found some glowing object at a hotel here in Seabrook?"

"How do you know my name and who I am? Where did you come from?"

"We're from a special unit which identifies the unknown and mysterious movements through our planet."

"I never heard of such a unit," said the baffled detective.

"Well Detective, tell us is this the first time that you came across evidence which happens to be glowing at any of your cases that you've solved here or in Boston, Massachusetts? The fact that they knew where he worked in the past startled him. "We would like to take a look at the object." Working many cases like this, we can know right away what you have.

Reilly thought about their question. He himself had no clue what was that he picked up. If they could tell him about the object, this could be his chance to move forward in the case, so he agreed, "Okay, I'll show you. Please turn off the light behind you, Sir." The light went off before he completed his sentence. Reilly was surprised as to how quick the lights went off. He reached his bag and uncovered a bright glowing object that lighted up the whole room.

Both men stared at it, and they looked perplexed. They knew right away what it was. Reilly overheard one of them saying, "She is releasing Set and Comet too. Oh, No!" Then they stopped talking, and the lights came back on. As soon as the light filled the room, the two figures were gone. And he still had the glowing object in his hand.

Reilly made a note of Set and Comet and searched about Earth Surveillance Unit on the internet, but nothing came up. He called the Brooks family, and their voice seemed far away not in Seabrook, it seemed. I wonder if they had left town. "Hello, Mr. Brooks? Are you there?" Brent pretended he couldn't hear him, "Hello. Is anyone there? I can't hear you."

"Mr. Brooks, is your family safe? You sound far away?"

"Yes, hello? We're fine. Hello? And the phone hung up.

After the call, Reilly started at his smartphone for about five minutes thinking about the case and the new discovery. He said out loud, "Who are Set and Comet?"

Chapter 32

—◄ ►—

Marc was now back home with his Saundra and Laura. Everyone was in a daze. Saundra was also still feeling guilty thinking about what decision would the Brooks make and how would they react after having seen her true identity. However, deep down, she knew that her dreams were coming closer to reality, and it was just a step- a hard step closer to going home.

To another who lives on the planet earth. With the Brooks family, Saundra felt in good hands. There is a glow in their eyes, she always thought. To her, their family seemed to be one of the forward-thinking families who were tolerant about the unexpected accuracies that surrounded them.

Marc was anxious. He wanted to call Brent to hear their decision and know his reaction. The cat was out of the bag now, and there was no turning back. It was spring, and the weather was going to be hot soon in Virginia Beach. Staring at the desks, Marc was thinking about a lot of things like the riddle that Amelia gave, "Uncle, is the lunatic a gentleman or an ordinary guy?" Then he remembered the lady at the gas station who answered the riddle. He was trying to figure out the meaning of the answer: "No, he is an ordinary guy who got a gentleman for a son since someone would have to be crazy to let his son become a gentleman before he's Achieved that distinction himself."

His thoughts then drifted to his daughter and her future and Brent's family. Yes, he thought, we are a "Moral Compass," wise lunatics for the next generations of Earth. Then Saundra walked in his room, shaking off his thoughts like she was reading them in the other room in their condo. "How are you, honey? Did you see their looks when they found out about us?" Marc Nodded and then said, "We have to take small steps with the Brooks family. These types of things can scare humans. Our timing is important."

Marc said, "I can't believe that Brent owns an Island and we have the blueprints to go to your home. What are the odds he would own an island? In this home state, where we live, in Virginia?" Saundra agreed. What do we do next? Marc spoke we need to go on with our life 's. Like this has never asked happened and wait for the next steps. "Saundra"

"Did you see the twins? I'm glad they're safe. Although, I'm still confused who would kidnap one of his sons and not ask for money?" Saundra thought to herself that this relic has to be recovered. She did not mention it out loud, but she knew it was a major cue for going back to Triangulum Galaxy. She then went out without saying anything.

After a while, the phone rang. It was Dr. Eugene, Marc recognized from his voice.

"Marc, it's Dr. Eugene calling."

Whenever he used to call, Marc tried to pay attention to the sounds and noises in the background.

He knew he would never hear such sounds again in his life. "Hello, sir. How are you doing? How my nephew Brent doing? Is he safe? Marc answered back and heard decrement in his voice. After the kidnapping he was more worried it seems about everyone more so his nephew.

You were right how all the pieces of the puzzle are coming together. Marc thought about the spaceship blueprints and the Island they left with his nephew… "Look as I was saying you're going to meet more new people from here and far away. Do not be alarmed there for protection and completing this mission

"I want you to remember this name along with a few that I have mentioned in the past, their organization is called W.S short for The Wildlife Syndication." Marc listened intently, and so did Saundra standing outside the room reading their thoughts.

"They have been around for centuries, Marc. They are going to be helpful, don't be alarmed. I think we need to call them." His voice crackled, "Someone kidnapped Jared Marc. I can't have that

happen again. I feel responsible for this sad incident." Marc froze when he heard a strange sound in the background like bees buzzing in a high pitch. Even Saundra was startled as well. She also had never heard this sound before.

Marc thought why Dr. Eugene is blaming himself. He lost his train of thoughts as he went back to the conversation, he was having with Dr. Eugene. Marc wrote W.S on a notepad there from many time periods in history. These members have their own purpose. I will give you a hint, eight animals. Also, please keep this information on a notepad for later use. I will be in touch. And you know how to call me whether I'm in Hampton, Virginia or anywhere else."

Then there was complete silence. Brent was staring blankly thinking about the conversation he just had. Saundra's thoughts were racing. She was thinking about what could she do. "Eight Animals," she whispered in a low voice.

Laura was sleeping in next the room. Saundra read her thoughts too, and she was happy that others knew about the Brooks' family. Laura has spent all of her young life without telling anyone who they were. But now she would have new friends who would know her for real.

Marc walked out of his office. Saundra pretended to be naïve about the call at first.

'Hi honey, you didn't sleep yet?" Saundra replied, "Hey, husband of mine, I'll sleep in a while. Are you okay? How was the phone call?"

"It was okay."

"Dr. Eugene?" she blurted out.

"Yes, how did you know?"

"I do not know. I knew I knew from these new gifts that I have got." He let her talk without interrupting. "Yes, I heard about this W.S. It sounds captivating," she said. Marc looked at her for saying this word. To which she said with a smile, "The perks of being married to a newspaper reporter, Honey." And he got it right away.

In Great Brittan, the Year 1939, during WWII lived a fighter pilot name, Sam Mitchell. He was one of the best fighter pilots around. He studied a famous aero plane engineer name Reginald Joseph Mitchell and Sam followed in his footsteps and studied the mechanics of airplanes. Right from the beginning, he had a goal to fly the Supermarine Spitfire single passenger airplane. He knew everything about this jet. It's wingspan, Rolls-Royce airplane engine (Merlin) and exquisite details of the spitfire airplane which could fly high in the air for long periods. The inventor of this plane worked for a locomotive train factory and studied that speed and ways of inventions can improve with time. Sam was admired

The R.J. Mitchell dreamed something more significant than his time. In all of his planes was a small picture of a tiger, and he had a tiger tattoo on right arm. He liked this animal; he knew that the war would end in a few years and thought about what would he do to settle down once it's over. And he was also an inventor of invocations in the area of aerodynamics. He liked being in the air, flying, and he felt out of place too.

He did his job as an airplane pilot for the Royal Air force well. One day he was flying over a battle country and landed. He was rebellious and competitive at his job.

Well, one day he landed his plane in a safe area near and private airfield and found a substance he didn't know about. It glowed in the dark. He thought maybe it was for airplane capacities. Anyways, he stored in flasks and never told one about it or why had he kept this substance for so long. He thought he better keeps this glowing substance, even if it's worth something, but he knew deep down to keep in 1939.

He fell in love once whole in school with a young lady and later he joined the Military. Other people seemed to gravitate towards him. Sam was somewhat of a loner. Anyone who knew flying the single passenger, Supermarine Spitfire, had to be confident of himself while striving to achieve his goal. Years later, he ended up at the desk of Dr. Eugene Brooks.

In Hampton, Virginia, Dr. Eugene got off the phone with Marc. He was thinking how his plan would work between his nephew, Brent, Marc and others who were involved discretely. He had just got back from the Year 2038. It was more advanced in human communication. The communication in 2038 and other ways seemed whimsical and hard to explain in the English language. He looked over his notepad of all the goals and people involved.

It was almost like periodic table, but Instead of chemical elements, it had futuristic words, like Vortex, Xeno, even a word from 1920's Hosty-totsy.

It was like he had studied each time zone and knew the latest trends of both past and the future. There were also the names of Starling Island, Tobias and his dog, Jinx. His notepad contained the names of planets, time periods where and when people were supposed to meet and certain times for an event to happen in favor of the plan. In events on the undisclosed base labeled start time (Space Police Agency). Hanna on base and Hanna in future, W.S Wildlife Syndication, eight animals, etc. There were many words and times and graphics that only Dr. Eugene understood. There was one more name that looked familiar, it was written in capital letters, SAM MITCHELL.

Chapter 33

———×( )×———

Takako was swirling in Noah's mind. He had seen the game for the first time. The process of the game, he thought the pace of the game was both fast and slow.

It involved members of the same team. Everyone was in space at the base. And how so much has happened in their time they there.

Hanna was talking to Harold about their new experiences. She knew everyone had a purpose here. "What would hers be?" she wondered. It was always her duty to be the anchor of the family, be there for her husband and children. This was her goal, no matter where they were stationed. However, Hanna wanted more. Thinking about the future, she could hear Harold speaking, but it was a blur as she was daydreaming about her real purpose. Then she snapped back to the present and listened to what Harold was saying.

"Yes, space bravo moon, we are supposed to train in this area in the next couple weeks. It could even take months," said Harold. Hanna shook her head not knowing a single word that he said. Harold thought that she didn't hear him before. As an understanding husband he repeated, "We are training in some unbelievable environments "April" Harold replied with her nickname.

She replied, "I bet. I also like it here a bit, honey. I still haven't gotten used to having any plastic. It seems like everyone is used to it or they're not from US."

"They are from US. Some come from other countries in the arm services but, most of them are from the US."

Then Hanna said, "Harold, I want to be more involved here."
"Huh?"

"Yes Harold. Looking around you in our new home. all of the devices, gadgets and appliances. I'm going be a different person on this unknown base. We were on many bases all over the US, and overseas, each base symbolizes its own culture. This base will change us all honey. We are already changed. We have been here for a couple months, and you and I still don't know why we are here. Have you talked to Colonel Mathews? Has he mentioned any road map for us, like Why are we here?

"No honey," Harold answered back, "I don't know why we're here, but I know in my heart that I'm going the right way. It's like I knew deep down we're supposed to be here. It's not only because that they have Dairy Queen here honey." She smiled. It was like this base was being purposeful, giving them some purpose. And they- the Johnson family were supposed to give something back too. Hanna thought, everyone seems to have their destinations here.

"It's a top secret but, I know you Hanna, your thoughts penetrate this base and all its top secrets. You have that gift to personify with others like an ocean with its ripples that reach far out and touch other people. I'm not worrying, April. Not at all," Harold added.

Hanna looked admiringly at Harold. She knew why she had married him. He was the Yin to her Yang. We could be called Mrs. Yin and Mr. Yang. Harold stop talking and noticed nothing but his wife. Only Hanna talking. Then he said, "Honey, I will ask Colonel Mathews more about why we're here and find out more details tomorrow. While I'm training for the Space Commander Moon, it would be better not to rush things, honey. They will tell us in good time. You think about my training about the moon now. They can call us the Honeymooners."

Hanna burst into laughter.

Okay, this would be our secret name while I'm training," Harold said with a smile.

Everything seemed well in the home. Harold remembered how this all started out for the infantry units here as he sat down with Colonel Mathews, he flashed back to that time the Planetary, Spaceborne, and the Planetary Marines Reserves (PMR)" Above and Beyond. He remembered what he saw, and he was told at the time to keep everything to himself. He retained most of the information of his training and kept his promise not to tell anyone about what happened. Harold knew that he was on a Space base, with three more units to be trained for. Harold didn't even tell his wife, which was a growing step towards staying transparent. His main purpose was to provide for his family. Harold went inside one of the rooms where he kept his paperwork about 'Operation Space Sahara 20.' As the base was very advanced, he doubted, "Are we in the year 2020?" He did not know for sure because there were no calendars anywhere on the base. No dates or year posted.

However, he enjoyed his training. Harold took the training more as a challenge just like his training with the Spacebravo Backwards, Commander Coleman, B.W. His next drill was with Commander Kristine Hernandez, Spacebravo Moon Division.

His thoughts went back to the Commander asking everyone what they thought about a "Moon Elevator" I'm sure it means like a building elevator but it for space to go to the Moon. That would be awesome. He had to wake up early, so he did his rounds before making it to the bed. Harold went to Zelda's room first. "Hey honey, how are you? I hope you are enjoying your new school."

"Yes dad! Our school is awesome. We have moved to lots of Army bases, but this one is the best one ever. We have made a friend already. Her name is Renee Wiser. She is cool. Renee loves Koala Bears, everything of hers has a Koala bears on it. She was raised here on this base. She told us. And all of us went to game too. It's called…umm… hmm. Harold answered like fathers always do, "It is called Takako. Am I right?"

"Dad, how do you know?" Zelda asked surprisingly.

"Your mother told me about this. You guys were pretty excited about watching this new game you've never seen before."

"It was a great Dad, involved a lot action, and there were Pullers, Runners and Flat Carriages. It was great. Nolan wants to join the school's Takako team, and so do I."

"You mean the game has both girls and boys can play on the same team?" Yes, Dad they can nice. Study up on the game myself to learn it so when you guys join I will be ready as a Dad. She agreed.

Well, I just wanted to check up on you, dear. If there's anything you want to talk, you can discuss with mom or me anytime, okay?"

"Yes, dad."

"Well Goodnight. We will talk again soon Zelda, Zelda."

Harold enjoyed saying her name twice. Now, get some sleep." He then walked out of her room and went to Nolan's room. Harold couldn't find him at first, all he could hear was Nolan's voice in the room, but he was not there. Then Harold heard an excited cry, "That Flat carriage is fast! wheeew weee!"

It was definitely Nolan's voice. Harold looked around the room and in the corner of Nolan's room was a section that Harold had never seen before he had joined his training. The top of the door was labeled as "Bamboo Immersive Virtual reality." Harold was amazed to see the unbelievable things. Nolan was in a small glass room and could see him running around yelling. Nolan was gliding in the air and landing at his own will. As soon as Harold entered the room and called Nolan, he lifted his headset off and said, "Dad, when did you come? I was practicing for Takako. I want to join the school's official team."

"Hmm, I see. I can tell you were practicing because I could hear you excited and running around."

"Yes dad, I was in IVR area where I interact with all five senses, (sound, sight, touch, smell and taste). I felt like I was there at the practice field."

Harold examined everything. "It looks cool. I will try this out later," Harold responded, "It's like real-life adventures." Gaming was fun, and he was flexible to try it.

"I came by to see how's the school going and your life here. Zelda told you meet a new friend." "School's great, Dad. And yes, we made a friend, she is cool. Her name is Renee." Harrold "Koala Bears I was told," said Harold.

"Yes, dad. Koala Bears, she has one on her watch and backpack and almost everything."

"How's school, Noah? Do you like your teachers?" "Yes dad, they are really supportive. I have the teachers in the school as well as in home, kind of like digital teachers. It's amazing and something that I never expected. In the class, all the people seem new here Dad. I noticed. They seem like no one knew each other or maybe it's just me thinking like this. After all, we're still in the introduction stages since we're new here at Apex."

"Well, take it in slowing and try to keep up with the homework first and then we'll see about joining the team," Harold advised, "I wanted check on you. to see how you're doing," Harold patted him on the back, "Okay son, we will talk tomorrow and yes, watch over your sister and listen to your mom while I'm at work." "Okay dad."

Harold walked, staring at the Immersive Virtual Reality (IVR). It was time for him to inspect his uniform and boats, he was ready for whatever the day was going to bring onto him. He looked at his name on the uniform and his command patch on his left sleeve which said Operation Space Sahara 20. He was ready for the morning and the morning was ready for him.

He couldn't sleep as he was curious about the moon elevator. He leaned over and kissed his wife and gently hugged her. Hanna smiled back.

Chapter 34

———— ⟨ ⟩ ————

Sitting in his office, Detective Reilly was staring his detective board, aka "Crazy Wall." There was a red string connecting all the clues together. He had on cue cards and photos and in capital letters saying Portsmouth Airport Hanger and also Mike Carter Helicopters. The Brook family was going somewhere. Where? He thought. Where were they going? Reilly picked up the phone and called Mike Carter Helicopters.

The phone rang about three times before the person answered the phone, "Mike Carter Helicopters, Can I help you?"

"Yes, I want to speak with Mr. Mike Carter."

"This is him."

"Hi, I'm Detective Reilly. I'm investigating the Jared kidnapping case.

"He's home now, safe, with his family," said Mike.

"Yes, I know, Mike. We want to find more about who did this. We're still looking for more clues about what happened. We wanted to ask if you can help."

"One second, Detective. I need to call Mr. Brooks before I talk about this subject with anyone, would you mind holding for a second?"

"Sure," said Detective Reilly, writing possible missing information on his notepad. He waited for Mike to call him back.

Mike called Brent on cell phone, "Hello Mr. Brooks, how are you?

"I'm good Mike, you called, is everything okay?

" Brent asked cautiously.

Yes, just guess who I have on the other line?

"Who is it?"

"It's the Detective that you hired to find the kidnapper for the case." Brent froze while being on phone as if the unfortunate incident rehearsed itself again. His voice was heavy. Brent was thinking what to tell Mike about the Starling Island and what they now know with Saundra and Brent. After a moment, he said, "Tell him we are visiting some friends in Virginia. It's okay to talk but no need to go into details."

"Okay. I will be to the point, Mr. Brooks. Okay then, talk to you later." Mike clicked the phone to the Detective. "Hello, Sir, let's talk."

"Okay, so you took the Brooks family on a trip out of town. What time did your Helicopter leave Portsmouth, NH airport Helicopter pad?" "It was around noon,

" Mike replied.

"How long did the journey take, and where did you go?"

"We went to Virginia. The family were visiting their friends. I do not know more information."

"I took them there and brought them back. It took 1 hour and 33 minutes to go from New Hampshire to Virginia."

"I see." Total time he noted in his notepad, 3 hours and 6 minutes. "Can you tell me where they were going to Virginia?"

"No sir, I don't know",

"Were they sad or happy for their trip? Did you observe their emotions?"

"They were happy during the whole trip," Mike answered, *"They had won the lottery. Anyone would have a permitted smile."*

Reilly nodded over the phone, "True."

He knew that they had just won the lottery for New Hampshire and thought this case was more than trying to extorted funds from their family. There were no clues of money being exchanged or asked for, which was kind of weird he thought.

"There were no signs of Jared being unhappy in the Brooks family," Mike added.

"Well Mike, Thanks for cooperating. I think that's all from my side." But as their conversation was about to an end, Reilly asked, *"Jared was kidnapped inside the Helicopter Hanger. There was no other family member around. What was so important that there was an isolated place on the helicopter hanger for him to be there by himself and no one else around?"*

Mike took a moment before answering this question because it seemed to be pointing to him as the person who had something to do with the kidnapping. He said, "I went back home after I landed. I have a wife and family, so after being away from them for a while, I wanted to go back home as soon as possible.

"What took place to the Brooks family made sense"

He a close family friend of the Brooks family. He thought to himself, Mike looking at the phone. His thoughts where. How dare you think this way?

"Mike," the detective said, *"Can I came there to look around tomorrow and just see if I find anything pertaining to the case".*

"Mike responded, "Sure, anytime."

"Okay, I will swing by tomorrow."

"Okay."

As soon as the call was over, he dashed over to his crazy wall to add more evidence like time, locations, traveling, etc." Reilly thought about the case and scribbled in his notepad in points, Helicopter hanger appointment at 2:33 pm. He kept writing, he glowing substance at the hotel room. No

165

money demands. Trip to Virginia to visit someone.

He thought how he could find the people in Virginia and thought if they had something to do with the case. There Lottery winners, so it would have to be another person, who is well to do too.

Reilly had given most of the substance to the Earth Surveillance Unit, but being smart he had kept a small amount stored somewhere else. There was a lab in Boston where he could go to look over the substance in himself. I'm sure the Surveillance Unit whoever they are they know more than I do. I too will understand the case and who is Set & Comet? It leaves more to investigate, he thought.

Detective Thomas Reilly picked the day and time on purpose it the same time and day the kidnapping happened three weeks ago. He wanted to see the surroundings of the location.

The Brooks were in the guest house. Brent wanted to go into the town to get to know the people living in Saxis. So, Brent and Nelson went to a place called Martha's Kitchen, a place not too far from Starling Island, and grabbing a drink he mingled with the locals. He met a couple which invited him over to their table. They kind of judged that Brent was new around here.

"Hi there, what's your name?" the couple asked.

"Hey, my name is Brent. I'm here on Vacations with my family. I wanted to know more about this area."

"Great, Welcome to Saxis Island. Many people come for vacations here like yourself. I'm Frank Spencer, and this is my wife, Susan Spencer. We live out here. You have an accent you're not from Virginia. You sound like you're from Boston, Massachusetts."

"Yes, I'm from New England. It's nice to meet you. So, tell me about yourselves, and how it is to live here on Island?"

"We can tell you about Island and the people living here if you have a little time."

"Sure, I have the time to hear." Nelson didn't speak much. He stood a bit far from them so that people the couple doesn't get conscious. He wanted be extra protective in this new part of Virginia.

"Well Brent, a lot people walk around here barefoot. It's a small island, a lot of us on the island get what we need when we want it with the population being so small and tourists. The schools are small Susan said. A lot of people who visit, the outsiders and tourists, they wreck our island. Some people at the restaurant heard what was being said and lifted their drink in the air to give a sign of agreement."

Once you live here on the Island you get used to small population," Frank added, "Whenever our people go to bigger towns and cities, they feel shy because they're not used to the outside world. We're not used to the areas where there is large population. And it will happen to you as well, Brent if you live here for a while." They both chuckled. Brent laughed too. He was listening very keenly.

Frank went on, "We have one police officer here or maybe two if they hired another one and a couple of teachers for the school. We get food and everyday supplies from ferry boats that come to the island at different times of the day." Brent didn't know what was expected from living on this island. but he was learning now and was amazed to hear what Frank and Susan were sharing with him.

Frank said, "There are different classes of people here, your either very rich or very poor here. The poor islanders like to kick it with the rich islanders to have more fun. Lots of people know and trust each other, so you will see a lot of doors and windows open. Also, the breeze from the ocean keeps our places cool. Would you like to have you want a drink? He stopped for a second and said shyly, "You said your name was Brent, rig ht?"

"Yes, you are right, that's my name, and yes, I will take a drink."

Brent thought there were some similarities and a lot of differences between Seabrook and Saxis like they would never leave their windows and doors open there. Brent enjoyed their company and thought it was time for him to leave, as he pretty much got what he needed to get to know the locals and their lifestyles here in Virginia. The people seemed friendly. He decided to head back home. Brent thanked Susan and Frank for their hospitality and bought them a drink to return the favor. He started his rental car, and while driving back home, he thought to himself Our lives are about the change.

And this would change the lives of those who live around us too. He took his time driving back to a guest house where they were staying. Before entering the house, he called Marc from his car, "Hey Marc, how are you? I like your state so far. I talked with the local people here as well. They're nice and insightful people. How's Saundra doing?

"Hey Brent, I'm good, and Saundra is well too."

Brent said, "We've decided to help because the Lottery has given our family a second chance and we want to help you have a second chance as well.

Chapter 35

―――――◦< >◦――――――

Yautja thought to herself, whoa this relic shows alot ranges to be in the hands of other beings than us. They wanted the relic, and we needed the relic this very rare. Set and Comet Kind of seemed speechless as Yautja was talking. It was like they wanted her to speak first because they knew more about this Relic. Silence from Comet and Set settled in.

Set stood up and brushed his white beard with his hands for about five minutes before he spoke. He then turned to Yautja and leaned in a little closer and spoke in slowly broken words, "Relics, are found in unexpected places. They adapt to whatever surroundings they are in. From time to time have fetched treasures.

Yautja sat down and listened attentively. Comet let Set give the wisdom to Yautja.

"These Relics can be dangerous as well, depending on the situation and the person who has it." Then Comet said something to Set in a different language. As an interpreter of languages, he helped Set pick the right word that Yautja could understand. Set spoke, *"Point of Compass."*

Yautja was confused, *"A point of a compass? What does he mean?"* Comet knew she didn't get this phrase, so he said another word in the language that Set understood again. And Set said, *"Assignment."*

Yautja, thought this relic has assignments, and asked, *"How do we know the Relic's assignment?"*

"We will never know the assignments of the relic until we're a part. Like when you freed us from the time capsule at that moment, we became a part of the Relics assignment. Anyways, Are we on planet Earth? How is time is measured her? It has been a long time since came here. Do you know how time is measured here?"

Yautja was lost in her thoughts. Her brain was flooded with questions. She kept thinking of the situation in which the relic would go into action and How many centuries has this relic accrued? When do the assignments start? Is there a start, middle and the end to each situation?

Set asked her again about the time. "It is very important for all of us."

Yautja looked around the area and forgot the vast size of the spaceship they were on. All of a sudden, two more figures came up to hear her answer, two mini-figures Boji and Eolu. So, she tried to put it in the basic terms. "Since I've been here, the people of this planet use clock, watches and devices to measure time. They use another item called a Calendar for calculating the days, months and years. One year has 365 days or 12 months in a year.

Every month has 30 or 31 days except one month which has 28 days every fourth year. Moreover, every day has 24 hours. And every hour has 60 minutes. And lastly, every minute has 60 seconds. That is how time is measured here." Everyone finally knew what Yautja was talking about. It was like they needed someone from their planet to explain where they're at and how their surrounding times work now. "I remember now," said Set.

Comet, nodded in silence, understanding their location. Yautja continued, "It doesn't matter where I go, France, London or Canada, the time is measured in the same way. Right now, we're in the US A."

It finally answered the who, what, where, and how they got here questions." Set- the bird-shaped figure investigated the air. He flew backwards, forwards and sideways inside the spaceship while they were talking. "I've had many missions here on Earth," said Set and then he took different shapes, not visible to the human sight, even Yautja stopped talking to notice. Everyone else was normal. They were not alarmed. It was like they knew Set could do this. Yautja looked Set fly and disappeared in the spaceship.

Yautja tapped a button on the spaceship which turned on a camera which showed the visuals of outside surroundings of the ship. The digital screens were displaying information about the ocean. There were five levels of the ocean. Each level had a diagram of the ocean. started from the top to the bottom of the ocean. Yautja knew the details of the top-level very well, from her countless missions. This was Epipelagic, which was the first level.

The spaceship monitored every level. The second level was Mesopelagic, and with this the screen mentioned 650 ft. The net screen read, Bathypelagic which was the third level and the numbers read 1000 meters and 333ft. The fourth screen read Abyssopelagic blinking the numbers 4000 meters and 13000ft and the last level was Hadopelagic. The spaceship stayed in the third level, Bathypelagic. Here the oxygen levels were deficient. Even the fish on this level were those who had tolerance for such conditions. The fish found in this level were Viperfish and Barracuda, etc.

Yautja was looking at the screen, and she was amazed how it could keep them alive underwater. This spaceship converted ocean water into oxygen.

Everything seemed okay as she listened to her new friends from different time patterns. She was tried to watch the screens and pay attention to what was being said. All of a sudden, she heard a voice, but there was no image. It sounded like Set was talking, but when she looked around, she couldn't see him. The voice was close by and was getting closer. Then, Set appeared before her eyes, and he kept talking. "How can he become invisible?" she thought.

Seeing her shocked, Comet said, "There's a lot he can do. I would be glad if we are on the same side Yautja." Then Set asked, "Yautja, I need to tell you more about the Relic."

"Sure," she said.

"We have been to this plane before, many years ago, this planet was inhabited by Native American Indians, he said, combing his hair with the device Yautja had never seen before.

"The American Indians lived here at least 10,000 years before Europeans arrived," he continued talking, "They saw and invented a lot of things. Now there are many Artifacts from these people being called the Native American Relics, like Totem poles, Dreamcatchers, Cerement pipes, and Wampum, etc."

Yautja listened carefully. "Yes, there are many stone artifacts like the Arrowhead which helped many inventions of future like swords, axes, knives, and other tools, etc. There was also the Storytelling tradition in Native Indian tribes. To know their history, "A lot of relic artifacts were taken and put in buildings for others to see. But, they belong to the Native Americans. Like a puzzle whose pieces are spread out throughout the world. Many are stolen through time, to complete a purpose."

Yautja froze. She spoke in confusion, "I had to take this Relic to open the space capsule and release you. You both were in the capsules."

"Who did you take the Relic from?" said Set.

"I took it from a family in New Hampshire. The Brooks."

"I wonder if the Brooks family have a connection with native Indians."

After much thinking, Set said, "We now have an 'Assignment'." Yautja knew that she had to take the Relic to Brooks family. Throughout the history of the Earthlings, relics have been passed onto many religious people. At this moment someone must be looking for this Relic? Yautja you are on this planet for another mission as well. The relic will show the next directions.

"Well, they sent me to this ship, and I did not expect to see what I saw here. Do you think we're supposed to move this ship from this location or stay here?

"I'm not sure yet," replied Set.

"There are more compartments to discover in this spaceship. It could lead us in the right direction. There a map room, I have explored a lot here on my own. Yautja explained, "It shows all directions of any planet. Whoever has the Relic, it shows them the direction."

"Wow, it occupies the object? It's a cool map room. Here on the spaceship. Have you ever been on such a ship?"

"Yes, we have a bigger one."

"Really?"

Set answered, "People must know there are many kinds of spaceships with various shapes and sizes. I have seen spaceships of all kinds, with different shapes and sizes." Set was an intelligent being; he had seen a lot of in Space.

The Chief knew that something had happened. He felt it as he paced the room. He walked and paused and walked again. Then he went to Rhonda to share his concerns. She could tell something was wrong just by seeing the look on his face. He said that the Kiselemukong spirits had surrounded him about something that had happened on the Wanaque Reservoir. "Can you feel that Rhonda?" he asked. She stood still listening what he was talking about and then closed her eyes. It was like the entire world stopped speaking to her and the Chief of the Lenape tribe.

Yes, I feel this is the Kiselemukong, a negative sprit. Something has happened. She thought for a second and then said in a whisper, "It's the Relic. It has disappeared from the Brook family. I can see." The Chief knew it before she did. He wanted her to sense what he had sensed many hours ago. "We need to influence this spirit back in the correct direction," said the Chief. Rhonda knew they must send special guardians to protect them, and they will take many forms for them see. "We must send them now, Rhonda."

She agreed, "Yes Chief, I will contact the other tribal members in the state and outside New Jersey to start this process."

Chief nodded his head and said, "We will not call them so that they are not alarmed. I will wait for their call."

The Chief kept pacing in the room, using his hands to talk and react to his thoughts. No one knew what he was doing unless you know were a native of the Lenni Lenape Tribe.

As he continued this dialogue, Rhonda watched and listened to him. There were times that she disagreed and spoke back to Chief in his plan. In their native languages. She said, "You must send Panda this way and the Tiger that way. It would be better." The Chief thought about it and agreed with her. He spoke kind of like the Nushetu means (Doe Deer). "Yes," Rhonda spoke back. They took hours of talking and planning. "There must be XASH kinds meaning eight kinds," he said. Rhonda agreed.

Chapter 36

—◀ ❍ ▶—

Marc was driving around the town, checking the place and the growth of the area while listening to music on his smartphone. He liked this area very much Two parts of the city kept the area trendy. There were two types of locals there, the ones who are born in Virginia and others who were raised here and from other states and countries.

Their families were stationed in the military, and Virginia Beach grew on them, so they stayed and started living here. Another reason Marc liked the area a lot was that one never knew who they might meet. Sundaraand himself were also new people to Virginia Beach. Sundara being from Andromeda Galaxy and him from Hershey, Pennsylvania.

Both were the first of a kind in the area. Marc was casually looking in his rearview mirror. He now had a habit of doing this from his experiences. Everything seemed normal. However, when he clicks on his phone to change the song, Marc felt that his phone was acting weird. There was a message it said it read in big letters, "Pullover in seven blocks, Mr. Dazet." There was no way he would do that. He thought someone must have got to his phone.

It's like it has been bugged. It shook him a little, but he gripped the steering wheel to make sure he wouldn't crash into someone. Marc tried to switch off his phone, but it wouldn't turn off. Then, all of a sudden, his steering wheel went out of control, the car was driving itself. He had never seen anything like this before, he was not controlling his car anymore, but someone else was. Saundra used to check up on Marc every half hour to make sure he's safe. She called, but it went straight to a voice mail. She redialed the number again it went to voice mail. Sundarawas now worried,

"Oh my God, I hope nothing has happened to Marc!"

Laura heard this and rushed out to Saundra,

"Mom, is everything okay?"

"I'm worried about your Dad, Laura. He is not picking up his phone."

Marc tried to regain control of the car with all his might and tried to hold the steering wheel all of strength, but he still couldn't control it. Marc thought of jumping out of the car or rolling down the window to call for help, but he wanted no extra attention from the public. His jeep kept driving. Two blocks, three blocks and then five blocks.

He counted so that he could tell someone when the time's right, hoping he gets out of this situation alive. A sense of horror came over Marc as the blocks went by. Then it came to block six, and the car took a left turn on into an empty parking lot. The car drove a little further and stopped in the middle of the parking lot.

Marc Froze. It was about 6 pm. He was waiting. Ten minutes went by, and it was just him in the Jeep and the parking lot. Then all of a sudden, his phone beeped and three black trucks came from everywhere and surrounded his car forming a triangle. Marc knew who they were, and he glanced upon their car window but no one could see through their windows. He was trying to figure out what was going to happen and suddenly the door opened, and there was a mysterious figure in his car.

"Hello Marc, nice to meet you. I'm glad that you made it here and drove exactly the seven blocks as we asked. A lot is happening. Do you know the Earth Surveillance Units?

We like to visit you to see if we're on the same page. Is that okay with you, Marc?

Marc was lost. He didn't know what was going on or what should he say or do. He could see a face in the dark purplish suit, baseball hat and dark glasses.

The man continued, "So the blueprints that we sent you are now going to come in action."

Marc responded, "I don't know what you're talking about."

"Listen, Marc. You don't have to be that way. We know, for a fact, that those blueprints are becoming more real in planning stages. As a matter fact, we know more than you think we do. However, I will play along and pretend that you have no idea what's happening. I'm here just to say. It's okay. We want you to put the plan into action. This is why we sent them to you, Marc. Aren't you wondering why we sent the blueprints to you at your office in Norfolk, Virginia?" Marc did not respond at all. He put his hands on the steering, so he was ready to move, just in case they take him.

"Marc, I'm going to give you something. It's a device. If anything, wrong happens, click on this device and it will contact us, and we will be there within five minutes. It doesn't matter where, when, how. We have our people in all places, and you still have my business card."

Marc nodded, yes, without speaking. He had never seen any such device before in his life. The man put it in front of him, on the dashboard.

"We know that have a friend with a lot of workforce and money that you would need for this project. We have to ask you to stay put. Just focus on the mission, take directions from the blueprints, nothing more and nothing less. When you're completed with it, we will be in contact and around. In a way you are a kind of like, what's the word?"

The figure raised his hands to express the word, "Yes, our ambassador. Yes, that's the word. This is all that we wanted to say. We don't have so much of a conversation but, from time to time, we show up in unexpected moments and do our job, making sure everything's okay. We will talk again, and you have our device too so we won't be following you anywhere."

It would intimate us for the emergency cases.

Marc was holding the steering the whole time. And then they vanished in a blink of eye. The car triangle moved in a circular motion and disappeared from the parking lot. Marc looked around the parking lot. And his phone rang it keep ringing. He picked it up. He was in a shock and terror so while answering he was almost yelling,

"Hello! Hello!?" It was Sundara's call, " Marc!. Honey, Oh my gosh, are you okay? Where are you? I've been trying to call for the last few hours. Where are you?" When she didn't get any answer a wave of suspicion ran through her, "Oh no! they came back! Are you Okay? I need to call the police."

"No! No, Honey. Don't do this. I will be home right away, and I'll explain then." Marc grabbed the steering wheel and drove off home, and the jeep was now in his full control. He looked on the dashboard and saw the device they gave him, not knowing whether to touch it or leave it. Marc was looking at the device while he was driving home. There was a green light that kept blinking. It was tiny. The device itself was black with a tint of purple. Marc had never been this frightened in his life before. People were looking at him and the strange light, but he kept his eyes straight on the road.

"Honey, I'm pulling into the parking."

Sundara dropped the phone and ran downstairs to get Marc. He turned off the Jeep and looked around to see if everything was normal and safe around him. He opened his door and leaned over. Sundara caught him before he fell to the ground. She supported his right shoulder and held his waist; it gave him some strength to stand up. She walked him inside and laid him on the bed. He had the device in his pocket. He hugged Sundaraas he lay on the bed. Sundaralooked at him. His face was pale. He said out loud, "I love you, Saundra." Her eyes welled up. Sundaraknew that she married the right guy at that moment.

"How do they even know, where I am and what am I doing, every time? Sundara, you will not believe what just happened." Marc said in a shock.   Sundara was listening keenly. "They control the Jeep. From the start till the end."

"What?"

"Yes, this was the third time that this happened. Whoever these people are, they have got a lot of people working for them here as they know all about my whereabouts. I don't know if I should call them good or evil, Saundra.

The way they appear out of no wear and vanish, it's extraordinary and unearthly. It's not that I haven't seen unbelievable things, Sundara." She smiled but was scared at the same time.

"This is not a pattern," said Sundara, "Do you think they know about Laura and me, honey?"

"I'm not sure. It seems they know about the plans only.

They have expressed no information about you. This was a bizarre incident. I mean, anyone that takes control over my jeep while it's still driving and brings it to a place and stop it on the dot a couple blocks later, they're not from earth. I don't think so, honey. I don't who they are. I just know that I love you and Laura. The whole time that I was there, I kept thinking about you two. Who's going to take care of you guys and everything. I'm glad we're going to leave soon. After what has just happened, it's even more important to me now, Saundra."

Sundara was looking at Marc and saw something unusual. A device. She thought, what's that device he has with him. Marc decided not to mention the device right away as he wanted it to be the last thing on earth no pun intended he would have to push, just in case. Situations go out of hand down the road. His wife knew that he would tell her.

She knew her husband very well.

"Do you think we need to move to the Island too, Marc?" Her question caught him off guard. "Well," he said, "This could expose us to the locals. I feel the chances of them seeing our family in its natural form to the locals surrounding the Island. All thought we live in a more populated in Virginia Beach. On the island, there is much a smaller and closely knitted community of people. We know that people talk in small towns, Sundara.

What if someone saw or heard about us building something? It could raise some serious suspicions." He thought about this subject too, while he was pulling into the garage. Then Sundara asked, "How are we going hide this from the locals, the blueprints and the spaceship, Marc? How?"

"I'm not sure of all these details right now, Sundara. But I know that others are supposed to help us with this project. People that we don't even know. This is what Dr. Eugene told me. And you know how to do impossible things, we have been together for a long time here, on earth."

Sundara thought about what he said, "It is true. We have been together in almost everything, Honey."

Marc added, "I was not there for Laura's birth because I couldn't come with you to your home. But now I could see where you were born and where Laura was born."

Chapter 37

━━━━━━━━⚫━━━━━━━━

Everyone was out of the home except Hanna. Harold was gone for his special training and the children for School. She had the home to herself so she tested out new items around the home and unpacked boxes. Hanna drank coffee from the new machine, she didn't have any idea how it worked but love it. She was sitting, sipping her coffee when out of the blue, a mail came through the tube inside their home there was expressed there. she was excited about receiving the mail on this undisclosed base.

It was just one letter. She looked at the seal in the back and turned the envelope around to see and saw something strange right away. It was familiar looking handwriting on the envelope. She did a double take and saw all the curves and alphabets again to make sure. She reread about ten times to herself and finally said, "This handwriting looks like my own." Then Hanna looked the sender's address. This was actually sent to Hanna. She thought it was a prank.

It said, "from Hanna Johnson To Hanna Johnson." She thought, it must be a mistake so she thought it had the right address here. It didn't have their address but it had the street address where the Johnson's were staying. Hanna was confused, she thought, "Should I open or wait for Harold to come home? What should I do?" After waiting for a few minutes, she impatiently said, "Well, I'm going open it and be brave like I am." So, she opened the letter. The letter was handwritten. And it was again addressed to herself and it started out with

Dear (Self) Hanna.

She kept reading, "Please do not be alarmed and take a deep breath before you read this." Hanna took a deep breath and then read, "This letter is from the future you to the past you."   She reread the first paragraph to make sure she didn't miss anything.

"At the moment, I know you're thinking this is a prank because this is how I would think. We are one so we have similar thoughts". Hanna looked around the dome to see if anyone was in the house. Hanna continues to the read the letter, "I think I should prove that this is me talking. So, first of all, Harold is our husband. He gave us a nickname which is 'April'."

Hanna eyebrows raised in astonishment. "How does this person know?" she said out loud. "We have two children, a daughter named Zelda and son named Nolan. You have been stationed on many bases including Fort Riley and Kansas. Harold is a good swimmer. We're from Nassau, Bahamas. We like our coffee two scoops of sugar and one table spoon of Irish cream."

Hanna believed that the letter was real and was from the future her because who else would know such detailed information except her husband and her. Hanna needed more information, a little more proof. She thought, "What this letter could do to win me over?" How wild and unreal was it. She kept reading, and her wish came true. There was something written in the letter that only she would know, not even Harold. "I'm a Painter," these three words did it. She had told no one that she enjoyed painting. At that moment, the letter dropped on the floor, it was emotional for her that she was talking to herself. The sender knew more than her.

Her future self knew what would happen after this undisclosed Military base that they were stationed currently. She knew what Nolan and Zelda become when they grow up. Hanna kept reading, I suspect those three words should do it, and prove that I am who I claim to be, Hanna. Hanna nodded and agreed, while looking around the room to see if something was about to happen. The letter further said,

I'm writing this letter to help you prepare and make a different decision to alter plans for the better. I request you not to disclose whatever I'm about to say but you may help your family by your actions. Hanna, this can work for all of us including me. Hanna was amazed. I know that you're thinking how can this be. I can't explain… just know that we are on military base have not seen before even the trip there, what you saw is unbelievable.

Hanna agreed with herself again. She thought this is crazy, "I'm agreeing with myself."

She kept reading on, First, I want to say I picked the timing of the letter to reach just you. I sent it at this time because I knew that you would be alone. This is the first of the letters. I will keep writing you to check in with you and share information to help you along the way. Keep this letter in a safe place and where you can go back to reread. Now that I have your attention, I would like to tell you that Harold will have two options to move to, in his military job. Hanna kept reading; you don't have to take my advice. I would have him turn down the first offer and take the second offer (S.P).

Hanna was curious, "What is S.P?" Yes, there's more, guide Harold. He will not be able to tell you much about what he does. I will help you with the translation of information. You're going be an inventor, be it clothes, building designs or shoe designs. This will be your field for the people of your time, my time and beyond.

Hanna was puzzled with this idea. "Inventor? Me?" she said out loud, "No way!"

To which the letter replied, Yes, an Inventor. I know you're thinking how could you be an inventor, but It is true. You would be an inventor of innovative ideas. The reason is that you can sense the practicality of people, you have a gift to see this side in people. Your inventions have helped me and many others. This all I can say for now. Hang on for the ride, Hanna.

Chapter 38

━━━━━━━━━●( )●━━━━━━━━━

D r. Eugene was sitting at his desk, looking at many types of screens, while his door was locked at the Langley Research Center. He was on the phone getting updates about the current events and progress from Joe from Rollins and Rollins. Joe was in Charleston, South Carolina, on his way to Starlings Island, Virginia to deliver the first shipment of building the spaceship on the island.

"Dr. Eugene. I'm not sure what you did for Interstate staff not to check inside my truck rig at the truck weight stations" said Joe.

"Yes, I know, Joe. Just make sure you drive to Virginia and load the truck containers on ferry ship.

They are waiting for you."

"I will, Dr. Eugene. I have to make seven more trips to this island."

"Good, I know it's going to complete half of the work of this mission. I need you as I did before for the base mission."

"Dr. Eugene, I have hired one more person to help me from Georgia. He is called Bull Dog that's his CB handle name. I will be taking his for help in this mission. We can get more done in lesser time, while I drop off the shipment, he will pick up one from the different given locations."

"I know who he is, Joe. I have researched every person that you hire. He helped you out with the wood in the Lowe's Contract in Seabrook."

"Yep, that's him. He's very fast and a professional on the road, like myself. Bull Dog knows the interstates and everyone at all the weigh stations. This mission seems riskier than the wood." "Yes, it is. Please do not break the seals on that truck until you're on the island. It's crucial." "I understand. I have about ten minutes before I'm back on the road. I will call you before entering the state line of Virginia."

"Okay, talk to you then. Be safe Joe and Bull Dog. Okay, we will, 10-4 good buddy."

"Dr. Eugene hung up the phone, still a bit worried about the transportation of the Spaceship material on the roads of the US interstate without being found. It was risky with all the truck transportation. He knew he had to do something.

He looked at the special locations of Interstate in Charleston, South Carolina from the special GPS that he had on the screen which connected him to Satellites and provided him information that he needed to help Joe and Bull Dog on the trip. He was on Interstate 526 in Charleston. Now the transporters were two, so he made sure that he had Bull Dog's coordinates as well. He calculated the distance between Charleston to Starlings Island, to be 535 miles about 8 hours which was not bad. He took a mental note. Then Dr. Eugene went through his notes about the manmade islands. First one was 'The Venetian Island, Florida' there are 6 inhabited Islands all connected by bridges.

Many people use to go there for a day to relax and rest. Then there's, 'The Palm Jumeirah, Dubai' which is the largest island made from scratch. It has 20 hotels and with over a thousand high-end villas and apartments. Palm island attracts lots of tourists and visitors. He kept reading and saw the 'Pearl Island, Qatar' spread over 4 million miles and has hotels, retail stores, restaurants, etc. Dr Eugene was amazed at the sheer size of the islands made to this current date. He studied the parameters and how each island was built to have some insights for building on Starlings Island.

Dr. Eugene kept reading while taking notes. The last Island that he read about was 'The World Islands, Dubai' It was designed with a lot of smaller island in the shape of the world map. Each island ranges about 12 thousand to 42 thousand square meters. Dr. Eugene was amazed at the size and construction. The World Islands included over 300 islands named after actual countries, Europe, Africa, Asia, North American, Antarctica, the

United Kingdom, California, Australia, New Mexico, and India etc. He thought to himself, Starling Island will not be in the public access, and the goal is not leisure.

Well, I'm sure the Island built in Virginia will reflect The Brooks family personality. Brent had two manufactured homes transported to Starlings Island from a company in North Carolina, called Wesley Housing Center, one of their homes was going be for their family and guest home for those who visit them on the Island.

Brent didn't know that his uncle was friends with this company before he met them. It was perfect for their living arrangement, 75 Acres was not as big as The World Islands, but it was enough for this project. Dr. Eugene knew he had other calls others to make. Everyone there was hired about Dr Eugene or hired by Brent through Dr Eugene.

From the ferry boat operators, truck drivers. Even Nelson was connected to Hampton, Virginia and Dr. Eugene. They were all more involved in the whole plan than Brent had thought. Dr. Eugene clicked on another screen and opened a file called W.S Wildlife Syndications. He knew little about W.S but was told through calls from others about it. They were already in the fields, ready to go. Dr. Eugene saw nine animals with descriptions below each of them. There was the Lion, Panda, Giraffe and Koala Bear, Tiger, Elephant, Parrot and Nemo Fish with the Orange and white stripes. Say they existed 1920 till 2052. Then there were long paragraphs under each name explaining characteristics.

All of a sudden, there was a knock on the door at his office at the research center. Dr. Eugene click on the screen right away…

To clear screen "Hello, come in."

"Hello, Dr. Eugene.

You have a phone call on your private line."

Dr. Eugene made sure that the computer on his desk was off and the paperwork safe. He walked to a special room for the call.

"Hello Dr. Eugene, this Colonel Mathews from the base."

"Hello there, how's the training coming along?"

"We wanted you to come down here, we're in discussion about having a new Divisional unit here soon, so I wanted to check with you if you are interested to know more about it."

"Sure, I can be there in a couple weeks."

"Sure. We'll see you then."

"Yes, Colonel Mathews. See you."

Dr Eugene hung up the phone and walked to his office thinking about all the parts of the plan. He checked his device to see the live locations of the 18-wheelers.

The Brooks Family was beginning to settle on the Starlings Island. There two new homes arrived, both manufactured homes were helicoptered in and shipped by water. This small shipping experience became a test runs for what was going happen in the future.

Margret Brooks couldn't believe that their whole family would be living on undeveloped Island. Both twins, could not believe it either that their new home was an Island in Virginia. Brent felt odd to be a lottery ticket winner when just few years back he was working at Lowes. Now, he was an owner of a complete island. The manufactured home had a new home smell. This home was temporary.

The Starlings island was not only to build houses but also to help others. Margret had lots of plans to decorate the new house and to be supportive to the family. Nelson stayed with the family as well.

"It was good",

Brent said, "I talked to the locals living here about this Island. We are going to have a family meeting. I want to talk about the Island, descriptions and all. We have the chance to read the welcome package now. Previously, we were too busy making sure our homes made it here on." The whole Brooks family gathered, and Brent started reading the description, "Dear family from New Hampshire, we have a welcoming package for your stay, 'The Island.'

Welcome to Starlings Island situated on the western coast of Virginia. We have between 75 to 90 acres of land here. The forest area is about 4 ½ acres, grass area about 5 ½ acres, and there also is a pine forest in the Northwest corners. We have few locust trees and cedar trees." Brent kept reading, and the family was listening to every word that Brent was saying, "We have well rounded diverse wildlife on the island, bald eagles, owls, deer, fox, raccoons, possums, voles and mice."

"This is going be new for us when we interact with the animals here," said Margret.

"I know, honey," Brent continued reading,

"This island used to be a major fishing hub, along with crabbing and oyster business. It was like a mini-port."

"It makes sense," Jarvis said. "I read cabbing is still big in the area. We can have more access to the seafood here, Dad," Jared added.

"Sure, we can, it's a great idea," Brent agreed.

"To east of us, there is a Saxis Wildlife Management Area of about 5,500 acres owned by the state." Margret said, "It's like the Wanaque Reservation." No one said it out loud, but they all thought the same thing, even Nelson thought of the three-letter word UFO. Brent continued reading, "The boat port is also not too far from here, and it hooks up about 80 boats. South of us is another island about 1,000 acres called Tunnel Island. To the North the Chesapeake Bay and the Pocomoke Sound. Moreover, there's also a village called Chincoteague Island close from Starlings Island."

Brent thought that this island's name sounded familiar. He kept thinking and then he recalled, "Oh yeah, Marc took his family on vacation there, I remember."

Returning to the topic, he said, "We have two guest homes, and we have to install a bigger 1000-gallon septic tank to handle both, the guest house and our house. There is also some advice on how to handle mosquitoes here. There's a paragraph on Mosquitoes Magnets. A warning about a weed that grows rapidly on the island and effects the flora called Phragmites. In the Welcoming package there is a suggestion that we can use the island for business. From Bed and Breakfast to a Retreat."

However, he and his family knew what they wanted to with The Island. The Brooks family was happy about the meeting and were ready to move forward with their lives on Starlings Island. Jarvis and Jared were excited to think about the adventures they were going to experience here. Brent had a warehouse modular built and sent to the island for storing the cargo containers that he was about to receive.

Jarvis and Jared looked around their new surroundings, Smiling and thinking the same thought, the thought of having their own amusement park which they wanted to build. "Do you think Dad will let us have a park here Jarvis?" Jared asked.

"I'm not sure, Jared. A lot is going on right now. I think he will but not right now."

A call came to Dr. Eugene from Virginia, "Hello Dr. Eugene. It's Joe here. We are about to put the first container on a boat to Starlings Island."

"Great, thanks for letting me know. I will text my nephew that the first shipment is on its way." "Okay sir. It's safe. I will make sure it strapped on tight. Bull Dog is 6 hours away for the second container. I'm going back out to get another. We are right on schedule. I hope for this to be a good mission from start till end."

"Thanks, Joe."

As soon as the call ended, Joe waved the ferry boat driver to go. Underneath the boat is where they kept the cargo. Most of the time cars travel back and forth. The ferry boat driver waved at Joe to move forward into the water, and the waves moved underneath the boat. Joe looked in amazement as the boat moved away from land because he had never delivered any package like this before.

Joe had some idea about the contents of delivery package from his previous missions with Dr. Eugene, but he wasn't sure what was Dr. Eugene going do with the cargo on this mission. This is why he made sure that Joe drives and no highway laws are broken. Joe then went back to his empty rig and jumped on the CB Radio. It was a private CB channel for just Bull Dog and himself, "Bull Dog, this is Eskimo Joe.

How's everything going over there? Over."

There was a brief pause, and then Bull Dog said, "Man, there's a lot of alligators on the road everywhere (Tires rubber on the road). Lucky, I got a bird dog with me (A Radio Detector) to make sure I'm on time." Bull Dog kept talking, "Yes, I went through about three chicken coops already (Weigh Stations). You can hear the traffic on the phone. Over." "Well," Joe says, "I dropped off the first cargo.

You are next. We may pass each other on the road or meet at a Rest A Ree-A (Rest Area). Okay I'm leaving now. Talk soon 10-4. Over." Bull Dog barked on the CB radio, his signal for saying talk to you later. Joe started his rig and started back down south to pick up more cargo. He was happy it was to be part of this mission and any other task that Dr. Eugene asked him to be a part of.

Chapter 39

———×( )×———

Harold was reading a booklet that he received from the briefing with other soldiers from the Spaceborne Division. The lights went dim, and Kristin Hernandez from Spacebravo Moon Division walked in, "Welcome everyone to your first briefing with Spacebravo Moon. I know you have learned a lot from the other Divisions. In this Division too, you will see and learn a lot." Then she yelled out "dim the lights!"

She had a Spanish descent in her accent. Then all of a sudden, we were all seated in a circle, and a hologram of the Moon appeared. It looked real like one could touch it. Harold had seen many holograms, but this one was more advanced. He looked around to see the reactions of other soldiers and everyone had the same look. It was very moving, all the sounds and the graphics as well.

The Voice coming from the intercom went through our bodies. Even the sounds were new for us in this room. The Voice said, "The Moon is the second brightest planet. When the voice said that Moon could cover the Sun and make it dark, the holographic image displayed the same changes visually. the holographic moon covered the Sun, and the room's light went dim and the light from moon radiated. In the space we felt like human giant, around the moon and earth holograph.

The voice said, "The Moon's gravitational pull affects ocean tides, human emotions. In 1968 The US was the first have man land on the moon. In today's time many humans have visited the moon on commercial tourist trips as well. We would show the future. For this room current times. We all looked around for current times. Then the earth appeared again. Everyone gasped waiting for the next image to appear. The words, 'Lunar Space Elevator' in bright letter appeared. Everyone exchanged strange looks. No one knew what to expect from the training. Harold knew this was going to be very interesting.

Then there was a cable of some sort leaving the moon up, and on this cable mechanisms an advanced-looking elevator was going up in digital format. It kept going up and on the top of that cable was the image of the moon. It showed many types of launching pads some from water in the ocean's middle, somewhere from land these moon elevators. Then the light went back on, and there was

Commander Kristin Hernandez, "Welcome to Spacebravo Moon." Everyone paused and clapped. Soldiers thought how advanced that was and that they had the chance to go on these elevators. Everyone clapped and stood up giving a standing ovation. Then she said, "At ease!" The soldiers stopped and went back to their positions. She walked by each of them like a drill sergeant, saying,

> *"This does not deserve claps. You will look out for one another on this training and this an order." "Yes, Ma'am."*

> *"No, it's yes Commander, not Ma'am. I am your Commander for this training of Lunar Space Elevator. Understand?"*

> *"Yes, Commander."*

> *"You will have a couple weeks to train for the Lunar Elevator."*

Harold look around the room and noticed something from the corner of an eye, a Tall soldier, who was the tallest in the entire room. He had a Giraffe Tattoo on his arm. In the military one could see many tattoos. However, this one struck out to be very detailed. The Commander kept talking,

"You will learn about different Life support systems, the ability to live and work in some extreme environments in the space. Different foods to eat, earth observations, payload deployment and weightlessness. This will include our training today. Please take the notes home. We will meet on Monday to start our training." Then she said in a loud voice, "Dismissed!" and the soldiers walked out of the building. Harold watched the tall guy walk out too. He had a long stride in the walk. Though it was ironic for a tall person to have a Giraffe tattoo and walk like one too.

Harold then went home shocked and happy about the training at the same time. He always wanted to be a pilot and now he was training for something bigger, going the Moon. He came in with a hug and took Hanna in his arms, "Hi April, how are you doing?"

Hanna noticed that he was home early, "Is everything okay, honey? You are home early."

"Yes. We had an introduction to our new training today, so our commander let us go home early. I'm home before the children." Hanna had a weird day, she wanted to share but decided to keep it to herself as no one would believe her even if she told them. She seemed happy about keeping it to herself.

"I didn't have time to talk Colonial Mathews yet," Harold continued, "I will see him coming Monday and discuss the mission on this Military base.

Zelda and Nolan were at North Apex High School. Having their lunch in the cafeteria with Renee. "Hey Renee, I liked that game Takako. I want to join the team."

"I thought you already did, Nolan. I saw you watching the game that night. It's fun."

Nolan saw Renee having just vegetables in her lunch. Zelda noticed too. She thought about their last lunch, Renee didn't eat any meat last time as well, so Zelda asked, "I'm not trying to be nosey, but there are only vegetables on your plate."

Renee answered, "I like vegetables. I get sleepy too soon, so veggies help me and give me energy. Anything with vegetables in them." Renee wanted to get more juice, and she told us she would come back in a while. As she was walking away, Nolan noticed, she had a bag with all stationary of the Koala Bear on them. Even her tennis shoes have a little Koala bear on them. Renee came back with something looking like orange juice and then she sat down and said, "Look, I may know someone.

I will talk to them to see if they can get you in Takako." "Yes, that would be great!"

Renee kept talking, "So, if someone comes up to you. At an unexpected time. Do not be alarmed. Just go along with it. Okay?" Noah agreed. "Well, we have to be back to class, you coming Renee?" asked Zelda.

"It's okay. You two go ahead. I'll be there soon. I'm a slow person here on the fast Military base." Both Zelda and Noah went back to their classes while Renee stayed drinking her juice writing in her notepad. She was the last person to leave the cafeteria.

"Hello Dr. Eugene, welcome to the base. It's been quite a while."

"Yes, it has been a while. How have you been, Colonial Mathews?"

"I am fine, thanks. We are in the third quarter of our training. Currently, we're learning a lot about new recruits. A lot of talented recruits have joined this time. I wanted to call you to update the progress of the training."

"How are the non-plastic based guideline holding with the families?"
"They're doing good. Some are having a rough time to adjust to everything, but they're doing okay as any family would do for this change."

"I have called you here to talk about a new unit called 'The Police Space Force.' Something new to overlook all things of space. We will pick a group from all of classes. They will defend space in earth's low orbits and beyond. All beings can join this unit with proper training. We'll have our own police spaceships, styles and earth's involvement with this new unit. It will help shape new space laws for all planets." Dr. Eugene liked this the new space unit. He spoke to Colonel Mathews, "I feel the rules and laws will change more when we explore more planets and galaxies.

Colonel Mathews agreed and said, "Now the new recruits are getting trained for the Lunar Space Elevator. I'm sure after the training I will take some new recruits and veterans from other locations, and we will begin the formation of the new unit." There only a few people who know about this unit. Please, if you have any more idea please let me know. I will do more research on new laws in the galaxies before we start.

Dr. Eugene explained there will be new laws formed. I'm excited. Well I'm going to head back to Virginia, I have lots of work about space too. We would keep in touch. Please, keep me updated, Colonial Mathews."

"Okay, I will, Dr. Eugene." Both stood up to walk out. Dr. Eugene thought it was a successful meeting between himself and Colonial Mathews. Many soldiers were watching this meeting to see how it went between time to time. Many knew that Dr. Eugene has traveled in many time zones and locations beyond what they would ever see. It was important to have this meeting with both parties. As Dr Eugene stayed on the base aliitle longer looking got file with some notes. He walked down a long hall punched some numbers to the entrance of this room.

He saw the records area. He waved his had over and it opened..and a Voice spoke from record area.

Hello Dr Eugene, the verbal notes in this area spoke. "Magnitudes Kept within bounds. Made out of energy and a protection". Dr Eugene wrote down the words waved his hand over the secrue area. He spoke to himself while he leaving the undisclosed miltary base. "Magnitudes kept within bounds" Made out of energy and a protection.

Acknowledgments

First, I would like to thank my parents for always wanting the best for me. They are the real Moral Compass. James and Edna J aka M+D.

Shirley Wiggerman an author I can't wait for the book readers to read. Look out for her books. She always there with insights and angles... (Dreams)

Nanowrimo 2017, and 2018. Every November their challenging writers to "Write."

My Editor: "T" Tatheer Fatima, One of the best. I'm glad our paths are crossing.

Book Cover Design: Valentina Pinovo.. Her designs are imaginative and gripping.

Book Formatting eBook & Book: Schedularr creative and the "Best."

Book Introduction: Manahil Waheed great writer with an impact.

Johnny (Veteran), Steeler Fan and Game insights for Moral Compass.

My Publisher: Austin Macauley Publishers: for their patience's and believing in me for a new book home.

Geroge Lester: Triple Threat Talent and friendship.

Lee Maynard: The Overseer

All Bookstores Independent and Major, Thank You for having our book series listed.

Mercia Hobson: Connection Newspapers: The coolest reporter in Virginia

Hampton Roads Virginia: There a lot a talent here from the seven cities, Thank You for the support and insights.

San Jose, California and Beyond

Thanks to God

ISBN 978-0-578-58361-7

Go Flavor Go

BFJ